IN THE SHADOWS OF NEW YORK

BY

MANUEL A. MELÉNDEZ

TWO NOVELETTES

Cover Photograph

by Manuel A. Meléndez

Edited by Charlie Vázquez

Cover Design by Carlos Alemán

DEDICATION

To my son Manny Meléndez, a true hero from the shadows of New York City, at a time when heroism is given to those less deserving, but as an FDNY EMT, saving lives, he is my hero and more than anything else, my pride and joy.

Other Books by Manuel A. Meléndez

Novels:

When Angels Fall

Battle For A Soul

Poetry:

Observations Through Poetry

Voices From My Soul

The Beauty After The Storm

Meditating With Poetry

Short stories collection:

New York Christmas Tales Vol.1

New York Christmas Tales Vol.2

Acknowledgement

It's a great feeling when a book, which begins as ideas thrown inside your head, is finally a finished product. And yes, even though the belief is that an author works alone, creates alone and at times secludes himself; that is a myth. We are surrounded by many souls who encourage us to keep following our dreams. For me, they are the power behind the engine that drives our creativity. They know when to leave you alone as they understand how precious your hours are when your juices are flowing freely. They are the ones who will listen to your ideas, even if it sounds like the incoherent rambling of a lunatic. They are the ones that nod their heads and pretend to understand that it makes sense spending hours, days, and weeks to come up with the name for a character who perhaps will appear only in one lousy paragraph.

They are my unsung heroes, and this book would not be complete unless I give the credit you all deserve...dealing with my insanity, you guys deserve a medal, a trophy, or at least a dirty New York street frankfurter!

The first name who always comes to mind is my mother, Angelina Veléz. The love in her beautiful eyes is what moves me to do my best and to stay on the right path. Then of course the second name is my son,

Manny Meléndez, a true hero at a time when heroism is given to those less deserving, but as an FDNY EMT, saving lives, he is my hero and more than anything else, my pride and joy. My sisters Lydia and Carmen and my brother José, they always make sure to keep me on my toes, and are quick to remind me if my head gets a little too big, that I'm still their little snot-nosed brother! *El presentao'!*

My brothers-in-law, Martin and Oscar, they also keep me in check and they will always be my true brothers from a different set of parents.

Next in line are my nieces Jennifer, Stephanie and my nephew Phil…my love for you guys is the reason why every morning, I thank God for giving me the blessings to be your uncle. And Skyleen and Izabella, watching you becoming two talented individuals fills my heart with joy.

In addition, Dolores, Hudson, Hunter and Juliet an extension of this great family that I am honored to be part of.

To Mary Lofaro, thank you for sharing and trusting me with your short story that became "Under the Hood," I hope I did justice to your story.

Charlie Vázquez, your editing was flawless and your friendship and conversations about writing is an education in literature by a true master.

Carlos Alemán, your cover design, like always, a masterpiece.

And now, the two names who overwhelm my soul, and make my spirit explode with the purest love God has ever created, Eva and Nikolas, my grandchildren. My love for you, my two little angels, is beyond words.

And last, but never the least, my deepest thanks always go to my Savior Jesus Christ and my Holy Father, the strength and the grace I receive every day is something I never take for granted. I am truly a blessed man!

Peace,

Manuel A, Meléndez

"LA BODEGA"

ONE

CAFÉ CON LA VIEJA
(COFFEE WITH THE OLD LADY)

He lay in bed listening to the abuse the garbage cans were receiving by the sanitation crew below his window. His wife of thirty-six years shifted her body as the springs from the worn out mattress cried old ignored complaints. Fixed his eyes on the digital numbers of the alarm clock radio. It was five in the morning. Slid from under the covers as silent as his fifty-eight year old body allowed him—his bones creaking with discomfort.

He stumbled on his slippers and regained his balance. Something crackled on his back. The room was dark, but at this stage of his life, he didn't need any

1

light to make his way to the bathroom. As he entered the small toilet, he heard his wife beginning to awake. Turned the water on the sink as a tired old yawn spread his bad breath around. Brushed his teeth, shaved, and took a hot shower — his everyday routine.

He opened the bathroom door and, as always, the fresh-brewed coffee greeted him like an old faithful dog. Slouched into the kitchen wrapped with the warm terry cloth bathrobe that his daughter had given him last Christmas. Towel-dried the last remaining hairs on his head while plopping down on the chair of the dining room table, waiting for his wife to place the coffee in front of him. Gazed at his wife's back while she prepared the coffee.

She was wearing her nightgown without a robe. No longer the thin shapely little woman he had married all those years ago. But she was still the most beautiful woman that his eyes had ever fallen upon. She swirled toward him with a smoking mug that read #1 HUSBAND.

Her hair was as misshaped as a storm-battered nest. Her face shined with the last residue of her cold cream. Sagging breasts jiggled under the satin gown—age and years of breast-feeding their three children. Pouchy belly hung low.

Don Pepe couldn't imagine anyone as lovely and radiant as her. After so many years she was still the shy jibarita he loved so much. She placed the mug on the table and kissed his forehead. He squeezed her soft drooping bottom. She slapped his hand.

"Dirty old man," she said sweetly, going toward the bathroom.

After a few minutes she reappeared, served herself some coffee and sat across from him. Her hair was combed back and her face wasn't shiny anymore, but fresh and pretty. They winked at one another, enjoying the peaceful dawn. Don Pepe finished his coffee, went back to the bedroom and got dressed. It was time to go to work.

TWO

POR LA MANAÑA
(IN THE MORNING)

He glanced at the quiet empty streets and their serenity beheld him in hypnotic caresses. A slow-moving car passed and stopped at the light. A pigeon above the yellow awning peeked at him with glass-like questioning eyes. A matted stray dog crossed the street; its ears perked up like antennas seeking better reception.

Don Pepe slid the key into the lock as mechanical chambers opened up with the resilience of an experienced, but bored whore. He lifted the graffiti-stained gate, its annoying screech polluting the stillness of the early morning. Stepped over a fresh pile of dog shit and cursed — out of habit. He opened the door, as the stale musky smells of rust rushed by. Scanned the inside of the store — again out of habit — to make sure it was empty.

Four years ago he had surprised a couple of robbers, which resulted with a bullet in his thigh and a hard slap on his head from a crow bar. It was a nasty situation that awarded him an unpleasant stay inside the walls of Mount Sinai Hospital.

Don Pepe made his way behind the counter and flicked the fluorescent lights on the ceiling on. Yellowish streams bathed the cramped aisles with brightness. He passed by the over ripened bananas and their offensive sweet acidic smell. His first loss of the day. Walked to the back of the store and grabbed a green hose that was coiled on the floor resembling a dead snake.

He turned the water on and dragged it to the front. Pressed the nozzle as he showered the sidewalk. After receiving various tickets from the sanitation flunkies for broken beer bottles left by late night revelers, he made sure to hose the front and clean the sidewalk before the vultures of the city arrived with their happy pens and even happier summonses.

As he sprayed he found himself whistling — again out of habit. Hauled the hose back to its hiding place and settled behind the counter with the glass displayed-refrigerator underneath. Looked out through the glass storefront, observing the calm streets beginning to stir with life. Clicked the radio on.

Spanish music filtered and carried its rhythms throughout the store. Poured a cup of steaming coffee from the thermos, which his wife always prepared for him. Sipped the strong Bustelo, preparing him for another grueling day. Glimpsed at the clock above the Sacred Heart picture — again out of habit. Even before he could focus on the tickling arrows, he knew that it was six-thirty in the morning.

He felt at peace and the tranquility of the brand new day whispered promises, which he knew, would surely be broken. He loved the neighborhood and it saddened him by the label it had received, a high crime nightmare. What a shame. Neighborhoods were not bad, but there were a few charlatans that gave a black eye to what the hard honest proud person strove to accomplish.

He found himself singing along with the old song that floated from the radio. It was a classic. Hummed the words, which he had forgotten. Unfolded *El Diario-La Prensa* — the Spanish newspaper — and read the early news of a city dying with no hope in sight. The street gangs were taking over the schools, and he feared for the safety of his youngest son being raised in the troublesome labyrinth of Spanish Harlem.

His wife nagged him more than ever about moving back to their beloved Puerto Rico, the enchanted island of the Caribbean. Even that paradise was tainted by the madness of a society twisting and turning into a sizzling hell. His wife, sheltered by the walls of their apartment, still lived with the naive notion that only New York was bad.

When in reality, neither land nor country has been spared. Society had lost all sense of living in happiness and peace. All were going at full speed toward a sure course of destruction and salvation was nowhere near. It made no sense, none whatsoever.

He was stumped on a word from the crossword puzzle, while behind him the clock ticked away. He felt tired and wondered if retirement would ever come. Perhaps not. He had become a slave with no master, but himself. He was pissing now more than ever, and he feared if some old age sickness was planning to ambush him. He would come around to seeing a doctor even though he didn't have too much trust in them. Fifty-eight years old and he felt robust enough to live another thirty years, hoping that God had the same game plan.

He raised his eyes from the newspaper and watched as a ragged truck backfired and rested in front of the store. In hissing protest as the engine was turned off. Don Pepe came around the counter and walked to the door as Miguel climbed down from the dented beat up truck. Miguel had been driving the same truck longer than Don Pepe could remember and he was always in awe that the old jalopy was still running.

"¿Cómo está, Don Pepe?" Miguel shouted, while opening the back. He slammed a rusty hand-truck on the street and began placing boxes on it.

Don Pepe approached the back of the old Chevrolet and squeezed Miguel's shoulders. "¿Cómo está, viejo? You are early today," he said, peeking inside at the darkened cargo. "What do you have for me today?"

Miguel stopped loading and removed a printed invoice from his clipboard. He offered it to Don Pepe. "Listen, could you use an extra case of corned beef?" Miguel asked, wiping his brow from perspiration.

It was early May and the morning was laced with hints of a hot and uncomfortable summer on the way. "I have an extra case and it's a pain in the ass to take it back to the warehouse. You know what I mean?"

"Sí...I know what you mean. But I still have the last case that you had extra from last month. Viejo, you have to learn how to steal better things."

Miguel feigned a hurtful look. "Ay, Don Pepe. Are you calling me a thief? You know that I am an honest working man. And by the way...I have an extra case of red beans. I'll give you a good price for both cases."

Don Pepe laughed and shook his head as he followed Miguel back into the store. Miguel was one of those characters that saw life as a big flea market. Anything could be bargained for. The man had a good heart and he meant well, but he was hitting the bottle so hard the past two years. Earlier and more frequently. It was none of Don Pepe's business to get nosey about it so he never brought it up. Each person controlled his own world, according to his own likes and dislikes.

Miguel deposited the cases of groceries at the corner next to the Pepsi Cola display. He wheeled the empty hand-truck and stopped in front of the counter where Don Pepe was already standing. "Want some coffee?" Don Pepe asked, as he put his reading glasses on to examine the bill. "It's nice and strong."

Miguel waved his hand. "With this heat the last thing I'm going to be drinking is coffee. A nice cold one maybe, but coffee, no hombre...not for me."

"A cold one?" Don Pepe said, faking surprise. "Chico, it's not even seven in the morning. Give that liver a rest."

The trucker grinned sheepishly as he counted the money Don Pepe handed him. He placed it inside an envelope and clipped it on the clipboard. "You still owe me for the two cases of beans and corned beef."

"But Miguel, I never agreed to get them."

Miguel blinked at him like a frightened mouse trapped on a glue trap. "You don't want them? I thought you were interested. Come on, I'll give you a good price."

"It's not the price, Viejo. I have enough of that crap collecting dust on my shelves. People have stopped doing compras in the bodegas. They'd rather shop in the big supermarkets with their double coupons and all that. If I sell two cans of beans in one week, I'm lucky. The corned beef, forget it. If I sell two cans in the whole year I'll drop dead from excitement."

"If it's the money you could pay me for one case today and the next time you can pay for the other," Miguel said, without listening to Don Pepe. "Come on, out of good faith. I'll leave the extra case here on credit. You know why? Because you are an honest man and I like you."

"Ay, Miguel. It's not the money. You're not listening. I just can't get rid of the corned beef. Not even the stray dogs want it. All those McDonalds and Burger Kings have destroyed people's taste buds, especially the young generation. Nowadays more parents are taking their kids to a fast food place for dinner than cooking a nice pot of rice and beans. I'll tell you...if you have money to invest, here's my advice. Buy stocks on fast food companies. They are the only places that are going to make money in the future."

Miguel smacked his lips with disappointment. "I guess that means you don't want them...eh?"

"Lo siento, viejo."

"Not even the red beans?"

"Okay, leave the beans. I could always have a sale this week. Buy one can of beans and get two for free. May as well compete with the C-Town down the block."

"There you go, Don Pepe!" Miguel said, snapping his fingers with enthusiasm. "You could have a double sale with the corned beef."

"Do not push your luck. Consider this my early Christmas gift."

"Christmas gift?" Miguel asked, his eyes opening wide. "Are you trying to work yourself out of my traditional bottle of rum and fifty bucks?"

"Fifty bucks? I have never given you that much money on Christmas plus a bottle."

"You could always start."

"Viejo…this is no fancy store down on Madison Avenue where they charge you twenty bucks for a roll of designer toilet paper. The day I give you all that loot for Christmas is the day that I better close the store and admit myself into a crazy hospital."

"Coño, Don Pepe. I think you are really a Jew trapped inside a Puerto Rican body."

"Now, now. There's no need to insult another race. To be cautious with your money is no sign of being cheap, but careful. ¿Entiende?"

"Sí entiendo, señor Pepewitz."

Don Pepe snickered as he slipped a few bills from the old register. Miguel accepted the cash, counted it, and rammed it inside the front pocket of his trousers. He seemed to relax slightly. He peeked outside and wiped his brow again. "I don't know, but I feel that this summer is going to be hotter than hell. It's only May and I'm already sweating like a pig inside a slaughterhouse. Le digo, a few more years driving that piece of shit and I'm going back to Puerto Rico."

"For what? To escape the heat?" Don Pepe asked, making his way from behind the counter to the putrid bananas. He grabbed the entire box and dumped them inside a large tin garbage can. Miguel watched him, fidgeting with a loose label on the handle of the hand truck.

"Viejo," Don Pepe continued. "If you go back to the island, you are not going to escape the heat. I could see in the winter, but in the summer? No sé. It's going to be hotter out there. It's like jumping from the frying pan into the flame."

"That's where you are wrong. It's not the same heat. Here we have all those projects and tall buildings blocking whatever breeze comes from the rivers. In Puerto Rico with the small houses and palm trees, the breeze is all around you. It's a big difference. Anyway...when was the last time you went to the island?"

"Ay, viejo. A long time. My oldest son was only seven. Now él es un hombre, so you could imagine. Hace mucho tiempo."

"That's what you need. Close the store for a week or two and go back to the island. Too much work is going to kill you. You have to take time and spend some of that money you are making. You better spend it now, 'cause it's not going to do you any good when you die. You are not going to take it with you. And forget about getting an expensive coffin with your money. Olvídalo…because the second you die your kids are going to dump you inside a cheap wooden box and enjoy your money for you. Te digo la verdad."

"Oye, Miguel. You're really full of joy and hope this morning. Why are you so cheerful?"

"I'm just realistic. But if you keep working hard and don't enjoy your money, at least put my name on your will. I'll know what to do with it."

"What? Buy me a nice expensive coffin?"

"You're crazy?" Miguel jumped up with a big grin pulling his face. "Just be satisfied that I'll bring you a five-dollar bunch of flowers from the Koreans."

"You are too generous...I'm a lucky man."

"Yes, you are a lucky man. Changed your mind about the corned beef?"

Don Pepe sighed and waved his hand as if brushing off a fly. Miguel grabbed the hand-truck and began wheeling it outside as Don Pepe followed him. The streets were starting to come to life as young kids bunched together with their parents walked to school. Cars began to move on the roads, exhaust smoke billowing. Buses roared by. Gypsy cabs searched for fares.

Miguel slammed the hand-truck inside the banged up vehicle, locked the back doors, and walked towards the grocery. "Bueno Don Pepe," he smiled, his gold tooth blinking in the sunrays. "I'll see you around. And if you change your mind about the corned beef let me know." He winked and stretched out his hand. Don Pepe took it and shook it strongly.

"You don't give up, eh?" Don Pepe asked, his smirk spreading wider. "Take care of yourself, Viejo. And good luck with that corned beef. There should be someone out there dumber than me. Cuídate."

Don Pepe watched as Miguel climbed into the truck, and in seconds, ignited the engine. The exhaust pipes faltered and shook violently. The jalopy coughed and buckled on its wheels and became part of the traffic flow in Spanish Harlem. The bodeguero entered his bodega and began to price and shelve the new arrivals of canned goods.

A slow march of customers shuffled inside. Mostly schoolchildren buying sodas and potato chips, a strange type of breakfast that made him wonder if they ate a nutritious breakfast before leaving home. Housewives venturing early in the morning with their rollers tangled in their hair and wearing flannel housedresses, purchasing Italian breads and containers of milk. Gates around the neighborhood rattled on steel rails, banging against overhead brackets as other stores opened for business. The pulse of the street singing its common song of sentimental hopes and precious dreams.

It was twenty minutes past nine o'clock when Don Pepe finished stocking the shelves. He started to walk to the back of the store with the ripped boxes when his eyes fell on the case of beans. He cursed without malice at the box.

"¿Qué se dice, Don Pepe?"

A booming voice startled him making him jump. It was Tito, an older gentleman with thick white hair and vivid alert eyes. He was the closest celebrity the neighborhood had to offer. Tito had played the harmonica for the biggest and major bands in Puerto Rico and on the mainland. He was quiet as a mouse and made Don Pepe's heart jump to his mouth whenever he arrived.

"Coño viejo," Don Pepe said, tapping his heart with his right hand. "One of these days you're going to give me a heart attack. Can't you just bang on the door or clear your throat, or do something? How about making the sound of the cavalry with your harmonica? Anything! Just don't be so sneaky!"

Tito stood looking at the storekeeper with crunched eyebrows. A seriousness transforming his face into a perplexed mask of thoughts. When it was no longer possible to keep the straight face, he broke into a hearty laugh, which ended in a coughing fit. "Do you know that you complain more than a pregnant woman?" Tito said, wheezing between coughs. "Why don't you just put a bell or one of those Chinese hanging things above the door?"

"Tito, if you haven't noticed the door is open," Don Pepe said, pointing with the pricing gun. The older man turned and examined the open frame with a puzzled look. He scratched his chin and grinned. "Well...put something on the floor that will ring a bell, or even better, ask Papo from the candy store what he did. 'Cause every time you walk inside you hear the sound of a frog."

"Now you want me to go through expenses just because you refuse to announce yourself when you come in?"

"Ay, Don Pepe...what do you think I'm doing when I say hello? Announcing the Second Coming of Jesus?" Tito asked, as he fished a bottle of malta from the refrigerator next to the counter. He stepped to the threshold of the bodega looking at the early day while sipping in slow swallows. "It's going to be a bitch of a summer, I'll tell you," Tito said, predicting as he watched two boys running to school.

Their shirttails already outside their pants flapping like upside-down flags. A stray dirty dog blinked from underneath a car with yellowish eyes. Its stare was blank and disinterested. Tito returned inside the store and dropped the empty bottle in the garbage. A little girl skipped in, her pigtails bouncing like suspension springs. She waited patiently by the counter, standing like a pretty señorita. Her dark eyes admiring her reflection in the chrome side of the counter. Her face taking funny shapes as she moved closer and then away from her image. She laughed, in her own little world of innocence and sweetness.

"Don Pepe!" Tito called out. "Hombre, you have a customer!"

Don Pepe shuffled over from the back, holding a pink-feathered duster. "What can I do for you, Lizzy?" he asked, walking behind the counter.

"Hi, Don Pepe," Lizzy said, removing a neatly-folded paper from the left pocket of her greenish, pressed blouse. She recited the contents of the list as if reading a children's poem in school. "My mother wants half a pound of spiced ham, half a pound of American cheese, a half a pound of olive loaf, and Italian bread. And a container of milk," she said, folding the paper and pushing it back inside the same pocket.

"And to please put that on her list and she'll pay you Friday when papi gets paid," Lizzy added, tracing her fingers through the top of the counter where it became the refrigerator.

Through the thick cold glass, Lizzy could see various cold cuts and cheeses. A few bars of butter, eggs, boxes of manteca and chicken legs. The chicken legs looked pale and dried and the first word that came to mind was 'yucky'. She made a face and wrinkled her nose.

"How are your mother and father doing, Lizzy?" Don Pepe asked, winking as he sliced the spiced ham in thin layers and deposited them on top of wax paper.

"My mother is still in bed and my father already went to work," she said. "My brother has diarrhea, you know the baby, and he smells bad. And my big brother punched me on my arm because I told him that Barbie wants to marry Batman."

Don Pepe pretended that what she was disclosing was serious and listened with the attentiveness of a psychiatrist. His lips curved upward in an amused smile. "Well, babies do that a lot Lizzy. I bet that when you come home from school, he will be okay and smelling better. And for Barbie marrying Batman, I don't know. Maybe G.I. Joe will make a better husband."

Lizzy giggled with her hand over her mouth. She took the brown bag from Don Pepe, thanked him, and skipped out of the store. "And tell your brother that when I see him, I want to talk to him. Okay?" He watched her go and wondered why she was still around when she should be in school.

Tito leaned his old frame on top of the counter and reached for the newspaper. He flipped the pages, glancing at each from top to bottom but not reading whole stories. Only the first paragraphs. If a news article captured his fancy, he would read the fine details. Otherwise, he was satisfied with the first few sentences, which informed what happened, who did it and where it did occurred. What else did he need to know?

"Te digo,hombre. It's getting to the point that if you wring this newspaper like a wet pair of socks, it will definitely drip blood," Tito said, turning the pages with disgust. "In the ol' days there were not as many killings and violence as now. ¿Qué está pasando en este mundo, compai?"

Don Pepe shrugged. He had no answers and he bet that nobody did. He was just a person that observed life around him without trying to judge. His opinion was as important as the next person. Nothing better, nothing worse.

The early morning dragged into midday and Don Pepe occupied himself with various tasks just to keep busy. Tito's voice was the background music for the day. The poor old man had no family, so the bodega was his sanctuary from loneliness. They exchanged short conversations where a slight nod from Don Pepe or a nonchalant 'uhhh' from Tito kept the talk from silencing.

Then the news broke.

A bulletin that shattered the laziness of the young day. The news took Don Pepe by surprise and made him stop and almost drop a large can of pineapple juice on his foot. News about someone he knew. One of their own had made the headlines. Pride was the last thing to taste its morbid victory of recognition. He came closer to the radio, expecting that his exasperated motion would make the announcer repeat the tragic news. The announcer didn't. Another old time song swayed on, bringing him memories of palm trees and the slender shy sweetheart that he married.

"Did you hear that?" Don Pepe, said shouting at Tito.

"Hear what?" Tito asked, with a lost look on his face.

"The announcer!" Don Pepe rushed to the radio. "What the hell did he say?"

Tito glared at Don Pepe in bewilderment. He noticed his friend's worried look and he knew something was wrong.

"It can't be," he told Tito in a low voice. "No puede ser. Sweet God, it can't be."

Don Pepe remained next to the radio as the last tunes of a bitter love song dragged itself to a sad finish. The reporter's deep and resonant voice cracked through the small speaker. He reported the weather like a mechanical record and Don Pepe hissed and looked up at Tito, who was standing next to the counter. After a short break the announcer returned. Don Pepe had heard right. He lowered his head and mumbled a soft prayer. A person had just committed suicide.

Someone he knew very well.

THREE

ALMUERZO

(LUNCH HOUR)

Above the tenements a lone pigeon circled a blue cloudless sky. The scorching early May sun baked the streets as if it was summer. The schoolchildren, inside a fenced schoolyard, screamed and shouted, bouncing with a wild delirium. They looked like prisoners as the protective eyes of teachers and parents scanned the playground and its surroundings with the precision of Secret Service agents.

Young dropouts leaned on top of cars bragging about senseless stories to kill useless time. Drug peddlers moved and did deals, watching out for cops. Unmarked cruisers drove by — not fooling anyone but themselves. Young junior high students paraded loudly on the sidewalks, dreaming about their coming teenage years that promised conquest of the world.

Bored housewives hung out of window guards, their eyes absorbing everything the streets below had to offer. Old caballeros sat on building stoops, reminiscing about eras long ago forgotten. In between inhalations of cigars and cigarettes, they wondered about what happened to Roberto Clemente. Some argued boisterously that Orlando Cepeda should also be in the Hall of Fame, up in Cooperstown.

All around were sounds of arguments and laugher. Curses and compliments. Hellos and goodbyes. Up yours motherfuckers and God bless you. The colorful rhythm of the heart that gave life to the charismatic streets of ole' Spanish Harlem — El Barrio.

The hot news spread rapidly through the neighborhood, consuming everyone with the speed of a hay-filled barn fire. What demons stirred in a man's mind to push reality past his limits? What lurked beneath the persona of a life gone wrong? What made the subconscious mind and the conscious twist and mix into a brew, which became a deadly cocktail of poison? When did the winds of happiness and hope increase their powers into maddening destructive storms? When was the right time for Death to knock at your door? And if it knocked, did you choose to answer its calling? Or was answering not an option, but an order?

Don Pepe asked those questions, first to himself, then out loud. "What makes a man kill himself? What the hell could make someone go over the edge like that?"

Tito peeled an orange and stared at the wall. Doña Fefa stood in front of the entrance blocking sunlight from entering. She was a large woman with a menacing glare, with a tongue ready to lash out with the viciousness and quickness of a whip. She squeezed a few tomatoes and threw them back inside the box, not caring if they bruised. Her permanent scowl much heavier today than ever. Not many people had ever seen her smile.

"Please Doña Fefa," Don Pepe said, chastising her as he leaned over the counter. "Go easy with the tomatoes. After you leave I might as well put them inside a jar and sell them crushed."

She frowned at him and walked away from the tomatoes without saying a word. Don Pepe was one of the few people in the community she abided to. "¡Ay...pero Dios mío!" Her overdramatic tone screeched throughout the store. Her hand over her heart. Her eyes closed and her head twisted upward. She had missed her calling from the theater. "Ese muchacho...and to think he comes from a good family! Pobrecito...he and his whole family were cursed. Le digo yo. Someone threw that whole family a curse — un brujo — a long time ago. The second he was shot when he was a boy...and then his mother dying — may God bless her," she said, crossing herself twice. "That entire family died. The problem was that they didn't know it. All the father cared about was what was underneath the hood of a car and the sister fell in love and forgot about everybody. Se puso muy high-tona. I'll tell you, those two...father and sister...they are responsible for that poor man's death—"

"What are you talking about?" Don Pepe asked, interrupting her. Annoyance slicing through his words. "That man's father died a few years ago alone in his apartment. The daughter was the one who found his body. That man never came around to see his own father, so you saying that his sister and father are responsible for him killing himself is wrong! Not to disrespect the dead but with his drugs and drinking, that young man killed himself even before he put that gun on his head this morning."

Manolo came running through the open door almost knocking Doña Fefa into Tito. Not that Tito minded—he always had the hots for the ole' vieja.

"Don Pepe," Manolo said, puffing, trying to catch his breath. "I'm sorry that I'm late, but you wouldn't believe the mess of trains and people all bunched up at 42nd Street. The cops are all over the place. It looked like a carnival, but nobody was laughing."

Don Pepe nodded as Manolo made his way around and stood in front of the counter. Manolo was a good kid from the Bronx that arrived from Puerto Rico six months ago. Miguel's nephew. Miguel, had begged Don Pepe into giving the kid a job claiming that work in the warehouse and even helping out with the deliveries was impossible. Manolo was an honest hard worker and with the encouragement of Don Pepe's oldest son, he attended night school to learn English and to prepare for his high school diploma.

"Stop stuttering and panting like an idiot and tell us what you saw;" Doña Fefa said, scoffing at Manolo. Her small eyes pierced through the young man with jealousy. She took pride in being the first one to know juicy interesting news. When anyone other than herself had the open floor and all ears were cocked to every word spoken, she took it as a hard slap to her face. She hated coming in second when it came to gossip. Invented or not.

Manolo took the cup of water Don Pepe gave him and drank it in one gulp. Some dripped down his chin. "I was on the train when we got to 42nd Street. The platform was packed with people running and yelling. Someone said that a lady had fainted and fallen on the tracks and that was the reason the trains were not moving. Then this man came inside the train. His eyes were wide open and his face was really pale, como si vio un fantasma. There was blood all over his clothes," Manolo said, stopping and looking around.

He saw Ramón from across the street, standing next to Tito and Frank the mailman, peeking by the doorway. "Somebody asked the man what happened and at first he just shook his head, crossed himself and kissed a medallion around his neck. Then he started telling how a man put a gun to his head and pulled the trigger, blew his head off. Everyone sighed and straightened up in unison.

"That's it?" Doña Fefa asked, snapping, bringing the mesmerized listeners back to reality. "We all knew that already. You aren't saying anything new!"

Manolo dropped his eyes and shrugged. Those around him began to disperse and with a slight abashed smile, he went to the back of the store.

"Never a dull moment in this city," Frank said, handing envelopes to Don Pepe.

"Coño, Frankie," Don Pepe grumbled, as he glanced at the letters and threw them behind the radio. "When are you going to bring me good news? Every time I see you, all I get are bills. Why don't you lose them once in a while?"

"You know that I can't do that. I'm just doing my job. Like they say—don't kill the messenger for bringing bad news."

Tito came around and placed his arm on Frank's shoulder. "Anything for me? I'm waiting for an important letter."

"Nope. Not even a return letter."

"You see Don Pepe," Tito said, "That's what happens when you grow old. Everybody forgets you."

"¡Ay Dios mío, Tito!" Doña Fefa said, scolding as she lunged toward the counter where the men stood. "When are you going to stop complaining about getting old? Look at Don Pepe. You don't hear him complaining and he's still working."

"Thank you Doña Fefa for the compliments," Don Pepe said, winking at Frank. Friendly confrontation was always healthy and good for a few laughs.

"And you," she said, pointing at Frank. "When the hell are you going to stop bringing my checks late? The past three times you have been late by two days!"

"Ma'am, I don't control the system. Whatever we receive is what we deliver," Frank said, defending himself. He'd been the regular mailman for the last five years and still wasn't comfortable with the old woman's brusqueness. He even yelled at her once, for her rough way of dealing with people. It had been a big mistake. She marched straight to the post office and filed a complaint, demanding he be fired.

Doña Fefa glowered at Frank. Her breathing coming hard and loud. Frank stared back, smelling her bad breath and cheap perfume.

"Hey Frank," Ramón shouted, breaking the tension that was building. "When are they going to have a test in the Post Office? I heard they will be hiring at least three-hundred more people by next year. Is that true?"

Frank turned to face Ramón. Doña Fefa, losing interest, walked to the back of the store where Manolo was hiding from her.

"I don't know when, but I'll tell you what. The second I hear anything about it, I'll bring you a form to fill out."

"Thanks. Hey Frankie, could you also put a good word in for me? You know that my unemployment checks are almost down to nothing. Soon they will be discontinued, so put a good word and move my application to the top."

"It doesn't work like that. After you fill the form, they will send you the time and place for the test. Depending on what borough they are hiring in, everything is done through computers."

"Come on Frankie," Ramón said, smirking. "You mean to tell me that nobody scratches a little back here and there?"

Frank smiled, his eyebrows arching. "Hey, I'm not saying yes and I'm not saying no. It may occur where the big boys are, me…I'm just a mailman. The lowest in the ranks. They won't listen to me, not even if I tell them that there's a fire inside their underwear."

"Frank," Manolo said, in his halting bad English. "Could you bring me a form, too?"

"Sure. But remember that you must have your high school diploma and know English by the time the test comes around."

"It's okay. No problem," Manolo said, turning to Don Pepe, asking him to interpret the rest of his answer.

"Frankie," Don Pepe said, complying. "Manolo said he's learning English and studying for his diploma. And that by next year he's going to be talking better English than you. And to watch out, by the following year, his Italian is going to be better than yours."

"Shit, my two-year-old sons talk better English than me. And I bet his Italian is better than mine, even now. I'm Greek!"

All the men laughed with the exception of Manolo, who stood looking at one laughing face to the next. Ramón explained to him what Frank had said and also joined the laughter.

Doña Fefa came out from the back. An angry look smeared all over her face. She hated to be left out, regardless of what it was. She huffed by them and left the bodega. That made them laughed even harder.

One by one they left the store as Don Pepe opened a small Tupperware and placed it inside the microwave. Manolo had gone to the corner pizzeria and Frank crossed the street to the cuchifrito stand. Tito left with Ramón. It was lunchtime, almuerzo time. The day was halfway through.

FOUR

LOS MUÑEQUITOS
(CARTOONS)

The schoolyard across the street was silent and still. Old headlines rustled lazily with the push from the weak wind. From the classrooms, children's laughter and the stern commands of teachers spilled out the window. At the corner of the playground, a piraguero sold his piraguas to those that were already dreaming about summer. His ice cones dripping with the sweet syrup that delighted the old ones as well as the young. A fire truck rushed by, its sirens wailing like a bratty child.

The late afternoon had taken a lazy sleepy stand and refused to become any livelier. From open windows, old Spanish songs crooned in soulful tunes.

Standing in front of the bodega, Don Pepe examined a young mother pushing a baby carriage. The tired sleeping boy drooled all over his little bears-print bib. The mother brushed her hair from her forehead and smiled at Don Pepe.

"How's the baby doing?" he asked, as he knelt in front of the carriage with the tenderness of a grandfather. "This morning Lizzy was telling me that he was sick. Is he better now?"

Lizzy's mother laughed. A timid and uneasy laugh. "That girl is too sensitive. Every time the baby cries she assumes he is sick. She should be a writer, because her imagination is pretty wild."

Don Pepe stood up, his friendly grin spreading across his lips. Lizzy's mother, Nancy, was a pretty woman from Brooklyn. She had married a boy from the neighborhood. They settled into his one-bedroom apartment and she got pregnant almost every year. By age twenty-five she was already a mother of three and the wife of a man that realized that marriage was more than just a warm body at night. Two lives already shattered even before they'd begun.

Don Pepe was proud that his children were following a different and more rewarding path. His oldest son, Gilbert, was a bachelor living on his own for the past eight years. With an excellent-paying job as an engineer and a beautiful girlfriend who was putting an end to his singles days. His little princess, Evelyn, who pretended to hate the term, was a schoolteacher and an aspiring writer with a book of poems already published. And Danny, the baby of sixteen, decided which college to attend and what to major in, tossing between medicine and law.

Looking at Nancy and her everyday struggles, and to the others in the vicinity, which seemed to have given up hope, Don Pepe considered himself a blessed man. He thanked God every day for his good fortune and admired his wife Sophy for raising three fine upstanding citizens almost all by herself. He waved at Nancy as she resumed her stroll.

"Don Pepe! Don Pepe!" a man across the street called out. It was Jimmy, holding an appliance he was ready to sell, as always. He crossed the street on bowlegged steps and stopped in front of the bodega. "How are you doing, sir? Do you need a toaster?"

Don Pepe scrutinized the used appliance. There were still burned crumbs caked on the inside grills. The cord hung like a dog's tail, sticky with grease.

"No Jimmy, I don't need a toaster. Besides, you know my rules...I don't buy stolen stuff. Where you got that from?"

"No señor. Without losing respect, but you're wrong. I didn't steal this toaster. It's mine."

"If it is your toaster, why are you selling it for? What are you going to do when you want to toast some bread? What about Pop-Tarts? You can't eat Pop-Tarts cold. You get diarrhea if you do."

Jimmy rolled that information for a moment in his drugged mind and smiled stupidly. "I have another one, so don't worry. Just give me five bucks and it's yours."

"Pero nene, for ten bucks I could buy a new one at the store."

"But I'm saving you the tax, hermano."

"No Jimmy, gracias. But I don't need a used toaster."

Jimmy looked at Don Pepe with disbelief in his eyes. He glanced around hoping to find a willing buyer. Scratched his face and returned his gaze back to Don Pepe. "Can I sweep the front of the store for a few bucks or wash the windows?"

"I'm sorry, but I pay Manolo to do those things. If you need money to eat something, I have some chicken soup and I could make you a sandwich."

Again, Jimmy appeared confused. He was hungry, but not for food. Itching badly and the hurt from the heroin demon began to arouse him within. Just a few bucks. That's all he needed for a quick pick-me-up fix. But to his disappointment Don Pepe, like always, was not biting.

After thinking for a while, he agreed for the food as he watched Don Pepe vanish into the store. Jimmy remained outside, swaying from side to side, holding the toaster under his needle-poked arm. Manolo came out from inside dragging a broom.

Jimmy saluted loudly, his drug-deteriorated teeth exposed by a big smile. "¿Qué pasa, bro?"

"En la lucha amigo, como siempre," Manolo said, as he began to sweep the front of the store. After contemplating his next move, Jimmy approached Manolo, his smile still wide and ugly. "Oye hermano. Can I borrow five bucks until tomorrow? I need to go to the VA Hospital and I don't have enough for the tokens. I promise I'll pay you back tomorrow. Look, I'll even let you hold on to my toaster. If I don't pay you back, you keep it."

Manolo studied Jimmy. He wasn't dumb and knew exactly what Jimmy wanted the money for. Even Puerto Rico had her junkies. "I'm sorry, but I don't get paid until Saturday. All I have is enough to travel from here to the Bronx. I'm glad that I get stuff to eat from the store, otherwise I'd go hungry."

Jimmy smacked his lips in frustration. He waved at Manolo and rambled toward the projects hoping to find someone that could use a toaster. "Damn, did people stop toasting bread for fuckin' breakfast?" he asked, as the hurt in his veins and body increased with the shakes.

"Where's Jimmy?" Don Pepe asked, glancing at Manolo when he came out holding a wrapped sandwich and bowl of soup.

"He left. He was walking in the direction of the projects."

"Poor man. Ever since he came out of the Army, he has never been the same," Don Pepe said, going back inside the empty store.

"So what happened to him?" Manolo asked, when the Don Pepe returned and sat on a beat-up chair that had belonged to a dining set a long time ago.

"Jimmy grew up in that building over there," Don Pepe said, pointing to a reddish tenement that housed a barbershop. "Then his family moved to the building by the candy store. He was a good polite kid. His father was killed in a bar over an argument about who was a better ballplayer, Clemente or Mantle. You know…stupid fights caused by stupid drunken men with nothing better to do with their lives. Anyway, his mother raised him and his sister by herself. The sister got married to a fellow from Connecticut and moved out there. That left Jimmy and his mother. He was a shy kid with not too many friends. Pretty smart as I remember. But after he finished high school, he was drafted and they sent him to Vietnam. Four years later he came back—wounded, crazy, and with the taste for drugs. I don't know if he picked up the heroin habit overseas or here. It doesn't really matter. The end results were the same. After coming out of the VA Hospital, he just hung out on the streets, wasting his life and money he was receiving from the Army. Some whack doctor claimed that he was not capable of working due to mental problems, and besides, he was shot when his whole platoon was ambushed. That shy kid saw a lot of madness in that crazy war. The bullet shattered something in his spine, which left him walking, like he does now. Not long after that, he began drinking and getting high. Before anybody realized what was going on he was always strung out. He became a junkie. As I understand, he had tried all those programs to quit, but the more places he was admitted, the worse he comes out. What a waste of life.

He would have been better off dying in Vietnam. His mother was so sick the daughter came around and took her to live with her. But they left Jimmy as if he was a dog with rabies, outside and alone. Those drugs are the demons of this society, and it attacks everyone. It doesn't matter if you are rich or poor, white, black, Latino, or anything in between. Look at the man who killed himself today in Grand Central. He used to live in front of the school. Came from a good family. Lovely wife and son. And for what?"

Don Pepe lowered his head and stared at the sidewalk for a moment. Tears of anger burning in his eyes. "You stay away from that shit, Manolo. Keep up with your studies and your dreams. We need more of our people to get out of the ghettoes and their gutters. We have to go out there, to the Wall Streets, and to the Fifth Avenues, and to the Park Avenues, and show the world that there is more to a Puerto Rican than a drunk hick fixing a beat-up car on Sundays. Or a goddamn junkie strung out in the park."

Manolo leaned on the entrance of the bodega. His face resting on his folded hands on top of the broomstick. Don Pepe rocked slowly on the chair's hind legs. Both men remained silent, engrossed in each other's thoughts, absorbing the life displayed before them. It was a hard life for some and an easy one for others. It all depended on what you wanted to plant and reap. Don Pepe had planted a seed a long time ago and was enjoying the fruits of his labors. Manolo was still planting and that was better than waiting for someone else to do his work.

"Are you guys waiting for the bus? 'Cause if you are it doesn't stop there!"

Mario's thundering voice and laughter attracted the attention of both men. "What's this? A holiday? Hey Don Pepe, do you pay that man to do nothing? 'Cause if you are, fire his ass and hire me!" Mario laughed even louder. "Vaya, Manolo, what's going on? Picking up enough phrases in English to go after las blanquitas from downtown? Just remember that lápiz is pencil, pluma is a pen, pollitos are chickens and chocha is pussy. And if the bitch wants more than ten bucks for it, you are in the wrong part of town!"

Mario yelled like a wild man as Manolo smiled and shook his head. Don Pepe raised his Yankee cap from his forehead and squinted at Mario. "Oye hombre, why are you so loud? You don't have any shame?"

"Shame! I can't even spell the damn word. How are you doing viejo?" Mario hugged Don Pepe and planted a kiss on the man's cheek. Don Pepe brushed him aside playfully.

"Coño Mario," Don Pepe said, rubbing his cheek as if removing something. "Are you turning faggot now? Be careful…if Chucho finds out he might cook you a dinner."

"No, we leave Chucho for Manolo. So he could teach him English, the type they speak in the Village," Mario said, throwing his head backwards. His roar of laughter was loud and contagious. "Talking about Chucho, have you seen him today? The bastard owed me some money since last week. I can't be playing his numbers and paying for them, too. You know, pendejo no soy."

"It's still early. He usually comes around much later. If you want I'll tell him to give me the money and

I'll save it for you. Unless there is another reason why you want to see him. Listen, I mind my own business. One man's hamburger is another man's filet mignon."

"Hey Don Pepe, let's not get fresh here. I am not as old as you, but at least give me more respect."

"Okay, I'll give you anything you want. I just don't want Chucho to come around and hit me with his pocketbook."

They laughed as Mario followed Don Pepe inside the bodega. Mario removed a little pad from his shirt pocket and slipped the pencil from behind his ear. "Are you still going to ride with four-thirty-five?"

Don Pepe thought for a second. "Yeah, and let me try my luck with three-fifty-seven. I had a dream last night that I was talking with my father and Sophy had a book about dreams and numbers. Whatever you dream about, there's a number that represents the dream. So the number three-fifty-seven came out in the book."

"You believe in all that mielda? You know, that voodoo and Changó business?"

"Listen, if we believe in the good—why not believe in the others? It's better to respect what you don't know. Why ruffle anybody's feathers?"

"You have a point there...talking about Sophy, how's she doing?"

"Like always. Nagging me about selling the store and getting out of El Barrio. You know how women are. They think that it's easy to just put your stuff inside a box and start new in some other place."

"Así es, you just have to let them talk. I think it's the best thing to do. Let them yap until they get tired or the next soap opera comes on."

"Don't let Sophy hear you talk like that. She'll cut your tongue off and make you eat it raw—pa' que aprendas."

Mario let out a faint chuckle as he swung at a buzzing fly. He missed. "I saw Gilbert the last time he came down to the neighborhood. I saw the sweetheart he had in his arms. Wow! Not bad. Anything there?"

"I don't know. You know me, Mario. I don't ask questions and besides, you know how I feel about wearing those monkey suits. But if it happens, I'll be very proud to have her for a daughter."

"She's white? Right?"

"Italian, from Staten Island. A very sweet lovely girl."

"Don Pepe, what happened? Gilbert couldn't find a good Puerto Rican woman? What's going to happen when he wants some rice and beans with beef stew? Come to your house?"

"Mario, love is not racist and besides, Gilbert always favored Chef Boyardee—now he got the genuine stuff."

Mario shrugged with understanding. Manolo entered the store and placed the broom on the corner next to the doorway. He removed two dollars from his wallet and handed them to Mario. Here, take my last two bucks. Bring me some luck, will you? I've been playing the same number with the same result...y nada."

"Well change the number. It's like a woman...if after the second drink she's not letting you give her some tongue, drop the bitch and look for another one."

"Nah, I'm staying with this number. It's the flight number when I came to New York from Puerto Rico. So far it had brought me luck. I mean...I met Don Pepe and everyone around here."

"Manolo," Don Pepe said, leaning toward the young man. "You also met Mario, the man that keeps taking your money and not giving none of it back."

"Yeah...you're right. I'll change my mind Mario. Let's go with one two-three."

"What kind of number is that?" Don Pepe asked, raising his bushy eyebrows and shaking his head.

"Another one that's not going to give him any piece of tongue, that's for sure," Mario said. "Bro, estás más salao que el bacalao."

"Fuck you!" Manolo said, cursed mischievously in English.

"¡Épale! Don Pepe, the kid is really learning English. Soon we'll have to get an interpreter just to say hello to him."

The three of them laughed, Mario's unrestrained roars drowning everything around.

The school had let the kids out as the street took a different magical transformation. The screeching from youngsters' throats filled the air with richness. The streets seemed to have awakened from its afternoon slumber. Now it stretched its arms and a boisterous shout of happiness was heard throughout Spanish Harlem.

Like small soldiers, they began to file inside the bodega. Their little hands groping the bags of chips and cans of sodas. Snatching Devil Dogs and M&Ms along with the Jawbreakers and Juicy Fruit gum. Their faces red and sweaty from running like wild horses on a lovely spring afternoon. They giggled at one another, while mothers mingled and gossiped outside. Young mothers and old mothers. Grandmothers and grandfathers. Big sisters and little brothers. Little sisters and big brothers. Cousins and friends. Bullies and shy kids.

The streets were alive and bursting at the seams.

Manolo stood next to Don Pepe behind the counter like fighting men inside a foxhole. They took crumbled dollars and quarters and dimes and nickels and pennies. Little boys with dirty collars around their necks and little girls with untamed hair that had been neat ponytails or pigtails. Like a swarm of locusts, the children entered, and just the same they left. Their wrappers littered the store and the sidewalk out in front. A legacy left as a remembrance of their presence.

Don Pepe joined Mario outside while Manolo swept the floor once more. The streets were still packed with running children and mothers walking back home to start the dinner before their hungry husbands came home from work. Mario watched the kids running and playing. He envied them.

"It would be nice to go back to that time and relive your life again. I wouldn't make the same mistakes. I would love to go back to the time when I was seven or eight, but with the same mind that I have now. Like that, I'm guaranteed in not committing the same foolishness. What do you think, Don Pepe? Would you go back to the time when you were seven or eight?"

"If I'm going to relive my life, why start at seven or eight? Why not start at the beginning? From the womb!"

Mario shot a twisted, revolting look. "That señor, I'm not going to even think about. It sounds a bit too nasty and just plain sick."

Don Pepe chuckled as he raised his hand and returned the wave from a woman four buildings away. Mario followed the shapely woman with his eyes as a wolf-like grin contorted his face. "Don Pepe, esa mujer está buena...fine, fine, fine." His admiration accented with a whistle.

Mario kept staring intensely without blinking his eyes. He didn't want to miss a thing. It always happened when he saw Elena. Elena was the most beautiful woman on the whole block. And the deadliest. She was married to a man with two jobs and no time to give her. They had twin boys that attended second grade at the Catholic school. She was always parading through the neighborhood in skintight dresses, which left nothing to the imagination.

Whenever she wore jeans it was like colors painted on her body. When she slipped on shorts, it was enough to lick the bottom of her shoes. And for that, there would have been a line around the block waiting patiently for their turn. Even the women stared at her, but obviously, not with the same thoughts as the men.

"Down boy, down. That woman is like an accident waiting to happen," Don Pepe said, tapping Mario's shoulders. "I just don't understand what her husband is doing. Too many men fall for that trap. They feel that the second the honeymoon is over, so is the courtship. Boy how wrong they are. Actually, the courtship should never end, 'cause when it does, so does the marriage. Don't get me wrong, the marriage could still be there. But I tell you, it's there for show only. It's no longer solid and will never be again," Don Pepe said to Mario, who admired seeing the old man in a different light. "How come you never got married, Mario? Or were you always waiting for a sweetheart like Chucho?"

Mario burst out laughing with no malice towards his old friend. "I never found the right woman, and to be quite honest, I always heeded to something an uncle of mine once told me. And that was to never take a woman unless you were going to provide her with better things than she already had. If she or her parents were doing an excellent job, then don't go and mess things up."

"That's good advice, but sometimes you have to take chances," Don Pepe said, lifting his cap and scratching his head.

"Yes, I understand that. But you should never take chances with another person's future."

"You have a point there, so you see, never let the white hair of a man fool you as a sign of wisdom. Probably the dumb ass forgot to wear a hat when painting the ceiling white."

"Or a sign of old age and senility," added Mario, as he peeked at Elena going inside her building. "But a woman like that, I'll marry in a heartbeat. Fuck what my uncle said. I'm pretty sure the bastard never saw a piece of ass like that in his whole life. Now that I think about it, that man was always drunk. No wonder he came out with that lame piece of advice. Shit! I was only nine. Talk about letting your life go down the drain for listening to a drunk. Jesus!"

Don Pepe chuckled and rubbed Mario's neck. Manolo came outside and took a quick look at Elena, who had come back to throw out the garbage. Don Pepe knew what she was doing. Performing her hot desirable number to her captive audience. "Wow," Manolo said, almost melting when Elena bent down to pick up a can that slipped out of the garbage bag. "Every day, she looks better and better. I'd pay big money just to have a pair of her dirty sweaty panties. Next time she comes to the store, I'm not holding back. If she wants to flirt, I'm taking it one step higher."

"Manolo," Mario said, instigating. "You can't satisfy a woman like that."

"Hermano, you might be right. But I'll tell you one thing, pana, I'll have a hell of a time trying!"

They cracked up like hyenas in heat. Each taking their turn salivating at their own private thoughts over the woman of every man's fantasy dream.

The small children were still visible throughout the community. Don Pepe glanced at his watch and went inside the bodega. He turned on a small television, which sat on top of a shelf he had built for that purpose. Every day without fail, he watched the cartoons. It was almost time for Spiderman, and soon his youngest son was going to be arriving from school.

A piece of fatherhood that was priceless. Watching the muñequitos with his children. A priceless moment, yes indeed. He had done it with Gilbert, which he remembered was a Speed Racer and Gigantor fan. Evelyn had fancied The Flintstones and Popeye. Now Danny, a comic book freak, couldn't get enough of Batman, The X-Men, and Spawn. Don Pepe looked at his watch again as he heard Manolo and Mario greeting Danny at the door. He smiled with fatherly pride and love. His wonderful children. Those were his muñequitos.

FIVE

CERVEZAS FRÍAS
(COLD BEERS)

Dusk, in her darkened outfit, sashayed in with the smoothness of a ballroom dancer. Starry earrings dangled in the clouds as her scented breath refreshed the newborn darkness. Spanish Harlem redefined the nature of what the day had once possessed and guarded, but now was under the strain of a battle lost so many times before. It surrendered to what the night dictated. No longer heard was the sound of happy children running, but the angry boastful curses of cars that rammed sanity into a corner.

Loud music blaring without concern for those souls seeking peace and comfort after a hard day's work. The vampires had awakened and it was time for them to take control. Let the children and the old ones have the day, but the night was owned by them. By the scums and the lizards that crawled out of hell. By the vicious lunatics that had forgotten they were once human beings, children even.

With a disinterested view of the shadows that blanketed the neighborhood, the pigeons settled along the edge of the roof. Below the yellow lights illuminated the stores along the strip of the sidewalks. A golden awning with bold red letters spelled out DON PEPE'S GROCERY STORE and in small letters stated the wares the bodega sold. Meats, Cold Cuts, Soda, and Cold Beers. Movie-house bulbs chased one another along the trimming of the huge glass window. Under the lights, a group of men sat around a small table slapping dominoes and chasing warm Bacardí rum with cold Budweisers.

The constant rush of buyers clutching the last ingredients for the night's dinners kept Don Pepe and Manolo busy. Late shoppers avoiding the trip to the supermarket, to assure that the meals were completed.

Tired workingmen carrying six-packs to enjoy the ballgames or the container of milk for their coffee in the morning. Young kids with their mothers, buying the last goodies of sweets, before nestling in front of corny television sitcoms. Young punks stacking themselves with their Colt 45 malt liquors and rolling papers for their joints. Worried parents grabbing cold medicines and aspirins for someone's sniffles. Clumsy young Casanovas tucking away condoms just in case they got lucky.

Don Pepe was exhausted as he instructed Manolo to rotate the cold beers with the warm ones in the large fridge that hugged the side of the store. Tito played the role of bartender to the men playing dominoes, making sure to drink a cold one for every two trips he took. Very soon the harmonica was going to delight the players and whoever cared to listen. Tito was a great musician, but the older he got, the more fuel he required to perform. Don Pepe's son, Danny, was still mingling in the bodega. Relishing the stories from the old timers and hoping Elena would come around. His young active hormones working overtime.

An older gentleman paraded into the store. His hand was limp and delicate, with a brown suede bag swinging on his shoulder. His black attire pressed and neat. His hair dyed in a reddish-burgundy color, combed back like a cheap imitation of Bela Lugosi. His face smooth without any trace of five o'clock shadow. His high voice more feminine than a real woman's. Even Elena had a stronger voice. But then again, she had bigger lungs.

"Chucho, come here for a second," Don Pepe said, as he walked to the back of the store. Chucho followed, his hips swaying from side to side. Don Pepe heard the laughter from the men out front and couldn't help thinking he was the butt of the joke. Mario was going to pay for this. He bet that Mario had planned the whole thing all along.

It had been mere seconds since Mario had left with a big grin on his face. Chucho's strong cologne was the first thing to arrive at the back of the store. "Listen, Mario asked me to tell you if you could possibly give me the money you owed him since it's almost

63

impossible for him to hang around until you come home from work."

"Ay, Dios mío, pero Don Pepe... ¿Qué le pasa a ese chico? He doesn't trust me or what?" Chucho asked, rubbing his hands as if applying lotion. "I mean...there is no problem with me paying him, but please tell him not to humiliate me like this again. It's not that he can't come to my house in the evening or on a Saturday. "¿Usted me entiende?"

"Yes, I understand. But you know I'm just doing a friend a favor. That's why I brought you here away from nosey ears."

Chucho glanced around to assure himself that they were really alone. He rummaged through the suede bag and fished out a small black beaded purse. He counted twenty dollars and gave them to Don Pepe. "Now please, don't forget to mention to Mario that I was highly embarrassed in the situation he put me into." Chucho returned the purse in the bag and slung it back on his shoulder.

"If it's any consolation, I'm also embarrassed. Don't worry, this will not leave this aisle. Don't worry," Don Pepe said, trying to ease the tension. "Do you ever get lucky? With the numbers I mean?"

Chucho batted his eyes and smiled sweetly. "I get lucky once in a while...with the numbers that is."

Don Pepe smiled weakly as he felt a rush of blood rising to his flustered face. Chucho threw a coquettish laugh and swung himself, facing the front of the store. Don Pepe followed with his eyes glued to the floor and cursing at Mario under his breath.

Danny stood behind the counter reading a comic book and glancing every so often at the small screen. The Yankees were in combat with the Seattle Mariners. From a distance, Don Pepe admired his son with a love that made his heart hurt. Danny had his mother's good looks. He was tall for his age, with intelligent soft eyes and short black curly hair that would make teenaged girls go wild. He was a sensitive child that enjoyed spending at least three to four nights a week in the bodega. He claimed he just wanted to help out, but Don Pepe knew better. Danny loved to be around him and most of all he marveled at being one of the guys. It made him feel older. It made him feel like un hombre.

"What are you reading, son?" Don Pepe asked, walking to the front and resting his elbow on top of the counter. He had always taken interest in whatever his kids were into. He had learned so much from them and they had learned a lot from him. A nice even exchange. Danny looked up from the comic book and broke into a smirk. "It's a new character called Resurrection Man...it's pretty cool."

"Resu...what? Whatever happened to the simple Superman or Batman?"

"Oh, they're still around. But this character is cool and different. He was a lawyer for the mob, but now whenever he gets killed, which happens in every issue, he comes back to life with a different type of power," Danny said, warming up. His eyes lit up when talking about a subject he enjoyed and comics was one of them. "Now there's another character named The Hitman, because that's what he is a hitman. But he only kills those that deserved to die. So now, The Hitman is after the Resurrection Man."

"Wait one second. I thought that the Resu...whatever his name is, was a good guy?" Don Pepe asked, confused.

"Yes, he is but—"

"Wait, wait, I'm sorry to interrupt you again. But I thought that The Hitman only kills the bad guys, so why is he after the lawyer that keeps coming back from the dead? You know, never mind. I'll stick to the normal stuff like a man dressed as a giant bat or a giant spider. That's a little more real than a hitman with a conscious and a lawyer that won't die."

Danny rolled his eyes with amusement and went back to the comic book. Don Pepe watched as Ken Griffey, Jr. slammed a homerun over the centerfield wall. Bernie Williams looked up as the ball sailed over four-hundred and forty feet away. Damn, the Yankees were already losing, but at least it was only the second inning. Don Pepe could hear the men getting louder outside, as the liquor began to take effect. Tito's yelling silenced everyone. The alcohol laced his tongue with extra weight. "Quiet now, this song I recorded with the Sonora Ponceña when I was twenty-two."

"When you were twenty-two? Who the hell was in the audience? Adam and Eve?" someone shouted, sending everyone into roaring laughter. Tito laughed too and without missing a beat answered the heckler. "Yes, Adam and Eve were in the audience and your wife was babysitting them."

The men's explosion became screams and raucous hollers. Tito waited patiently for the tiny whimpers of the dying laughter to subside. He removed a handsome gold-plated harmonica from his shirt pocket. Everyone turned their attention to him as he moistened his lips and closed his eyes. Ramon pulled his chair closer to the table and began slapping his cupped hands with a slow timing tempo. Now Tito began to play.

The harmonica's piercing melody rose and fell with the uncanny sadness of nostalgia. The tunes soared above the roofs, much higher than any bird had ever flown. The music filled the air with a magical sweetness as it tickled and softened the hardest hearts. Young thugs with their heavily made-up girlfriends stopped and noticed their grandparents' symphonies.

A symphony from the past that sounded new and refreshing. As refreshing as a springtime shower. As refreshing as young innocent love. The harmonica aroused the senses and brought forth a unique passion that charmed the soul.

Ramon slapped his hands on the table. He searched for the stars while his rhythm kept time in precise perfection. Tito bent his body backwards and rocked forward. Sweat poured from underneath his straw hat. His cheeks expanded and deflated in one single motion.

Don Pepe stood in the doorway with his arm around Danny's shoulders. Cherishing the quality time he was spending with his son, wondering if Danny was capturing and treasuring this wonderful moment like he was.

The smiling, content faces of tough macho men with misty eyes twinkled like small holy angels. Old-timers relived a time that seemed so long forgotten. Ancient times that had been buried under the burden of years, now dug out and bringing smiles and happy tears to their old wrinkled faces.

Tito played with a fervor that drove the small gathered crowd into frenzy. The harmonica's voice wailed its loving cry of love and broken hearts. It brought forth the spirits of a time when grandparents were kids madly in love and confused about life. It rose and entered the ears of each ancient god, and became the anthem of the gutters and alleys and streets and empty lots of Spanish Harlem. Tito played without stopping. He was on the fancy stages of yesterday in front of well-dressed couples. Once again, he was underneath the hot lights of television studios, waiting to be announced. To step onto gaudy stages as maddening applause slapped his back. Tito played until the last note came to a chilling soulful end.

The cheers were thunderous and the whistles erupted like volcanoes all over the neighborhood. Tito took a well-deserved bow and his broad smile shone brightly at the moon. His happiness danced around his heart and his humbleness shed tiny tears at the corners of his eyes. He mumbled a weak thank you and went inside the bodega to compose himself, while the praises outside refused to come to an end.

"Cervezas frías for everyone!" someone shouted.

SIX

BISTEC CON CEBOLLA Y ARROZ
(STEAK WITH ONIONS AND RICE)

Stale, flat air came in from the East River. A feeble breeze brushed the trees without much force, crashing gates secured stores for the night, daring anyone to break their stronghold. Speeding squad cars cut through halting traffic in desperate chases to the unknown. Distant bangs that sounded like thunder even though there was no forecast of rain. Perhaps it came from stupid troublemakers preparing for the Fourth of July, although the true El Barrio natives knew they were gunshots. Young punks with vicious pit bulls bopped down the street with puffed-out chests. Staggering drunks dragged themselves through parked cars trying to avoid the unavoidable fall. Hardworking laborers returned home from extra over-time hours, which only Uncle Sam would see. Booming speakers exploded from fast cars that shook the neighborhood like earthquakes. The metamorphosis of a family-oriented community had been taken over by the creatures that the pitch-blackness tended to spawn.

Don Pepe rested by the doorway mesmerized by how within hours, a beautiful painted masterpiece could transform itself into a hideous hellish scene. Behind him, Manolo attended the few customers inside. Those shoppers that trickled in and out, which always added a few extra bucks to the register. Danny did his homework and munched on his second alcapurria. He had already eaten a ham and cheese sandwich.

"Kid must have a tapeworm or something," Don Pepe sighed. "Boy could eat, yet he always remains slim. The beauty of the metabolism of a healthy active athletic teenager. They move so fast, the fat from the food doesn't have a chance to stick to their bones."

Diagonal to the bodega, in the building where Doña Fefa lived, Don Pepe followed a young man, descending the small steps of the stoop and strolling toward him. It was Freddy, a nice kid in his early twenties that sang in a salsa band. Forever pursuing a dream that at this moment was not lining his pockets too well. He favored dressing in black and his hair was slicked back, ending in a ponytail. He resembled a jazz musician more than a salsa singer.

His band had performed the last two block parties, which the community held every year. Always close to the Puerto Rican Day Parade. Freddy had a good strong voice that reached high and low notes with ease. The band was crisp and tight. It was a surprise they were still bouncing from weddings, Sweet Sixteen, and the dangerous after-hours places.

"Don Pepe, how're you doing?" Freddy asked, extending his hand. Always a polite and respectful young man. "Do you believe that man at Forty-Second?" He whistled in disbelief. "Killing himself during the beginning of rush hour."

"Would it have been different if he had done it a little bit later?"

"I didn't mean it like that," Freddy said, waving his hands in front of his chest. "I just can't believe what happened. I remembered him. Not that well, but I have a mental picture of him. You knew him well, right?"

"Sadly, but yes. I saw that kid grow up right inside the schoolyard. Always playing stickball. No matter if it was sunny, rainy, cold or hot. He didn't care. If someone was around to play with him, he was ready. Even by himself, he would spend hours throwing the ball against the wall. What a shame," Don Pepe said, shaking his head and staring at the dark schoolyard where he could see the glowing of cigarettes or God-knows-what-else being smoked. Lighting the darkness like steady fireflies.

"Hola, Freddy. Are you singing tonight?" Elena's voice made both men turn around like comical wind-dolls. Her big smile teasing even without trying. "I see that you are all dressed up. You look like Zorro...where's the sword?" She laughed a little. Like a little girl. Her fresh clean scent sweetening the old sweaty smell of the bodega.

"We're doing a showcase at a catering hall in Queens," Freddy said, turning toward her, his eyes behind his shades ogling.

"What's that?" she asked, coming closer. "It sounds like you're going to a game show."

"No, no. It's not a game show," Freddy said, rolling his eyes, hidden by Ray Ban imitations he'd bought in Chinatown for ten bucks. "A showcase is where a few bands play a medley of their songs for an audience of couples looking for a band for their wedding reception. It's like an audition or an interview for a gig or two."

"Does that work?" Don Pepe asked, feeling Danny's wide-open eyes through the glass window.

"Sure, if you perform well. Some of these cases could land you from four to five dates, depending how many couples are present. One time there were six couples and they all hired us on the spot. The other bands were pissed off, but they understood that it's part of the business. Besides they knew that we were good...coño...we blew them out. Some of their own musicians were handing out their phone numbers to us in case we ever need fill-ins for a night."

"You guys should sign with a big company...you know. Like Fania or one of those other recording places," Elena said, brushing her slender fingers on Freddy's arm.

"It's not that easy," Freddy said, acknowledging her touch with a smirk. "Everything is connected. And even if you make it, you're still trapped in the cuchifrito circuit."

"Cuchifrito circuit? What the hell is that?" Don Pepe asked, glancing at Freddy and not approving of the little hanky-panky he was having with Elena.

"That's just a term salsa musicians use to describe the constant gigs in the same little nightclubs for a few dollars, regardless if you are a recording band or not."

"At least it's steady work. That's what you want, right?" Don Pepe asked, trying to understand the musician's life through Freddy's eyes.

"Sure, that's what we want...but the money should be a little bit better so bands don't have to be running around on weekends trying to hit as many as three clubs a night. It's not like the American music. One catchy tune and they're suddenly riding in limos and selecting where and when to perform. Why do you think there are more one-hit wonders in the American hit list than in the Spanish one? We have to pay our dues over and over. There must be an explanation why Celia Cruz or Tito Puente still takes the gigs in packed sweaty clubs. Come on...those two are the equivalent or even better than Frank Sinatra and Aretha Franklin."

"Oye Freddy...do I hear some anger there?" Don Pepe asked, leaning on the glass storefront. "So if you see what's going on....then why don't you make your own label? Do your own recordings. Sell tapes whenever the band plays."

"A man tried that sometime in the eighties. He was blackballed from every joint in town. His career was over before it even started."

"Who was this guy?" Elena asked, admiring her reflection on the large window. She tucked her blouse deeper inside her jeans, revealing more of her cleavage.

"His name was Ángel Canales or something like that," Freddy said, removing his shades and sliding them inside his shirt pocket. His eyes sparkled like water droplets. "But what the hell...sometimes you just have to play for the love of the music and whatever happens it's going to happen. As long as you have good friends that care for you, the rest is just background scenery. Am I right, Don Pepe?"

"Sí hijo, you're right. Stay with those beliefs and if God permits, you will make it."

Headlights of screeching cars bathed them as they brought the conversation to a halt. Elena entered the bodega, followed by Freddy's stare. Don Pepe looked at the young man sternly and gave him a fatherly frown. Freddy's eyebrows arched up as an innocent, I'm-not-doing-anything-wrong look spread all over his handsome chiseled features.

"Don Pepe," Freddy said, placing his hand on the older man's shoulder. To establish privacy between them. "I was wondering if you could lend me a few bucks until Sunday. I have a wedding on Saturday, so I'll be able to pay you back."

"Sure hijo, ¿cómo no? How much do you need?"

"I don't know. Ten? Maybe twenty?"

"How's this? Here's forty. At least it will keep you honest until the wedding. If you need anything from the store we could always work something out. Okay?"

"Gracias señor, gracias," Freddy said, taking the two twenty-dollar bills and putting them inside his wallet. "Listen, I have to catch a train to Astoria. I should be leaving now."

"Want me to fix you a sandwich? You will sound better with a full stomach."

"Wow! Don Pepe, you're a saint. Gracias," Freddy said, leading Don Pepe inside the bodega.

Elena stood by the counter flipping through the pages of *TV Guide*. Manolo grinned from ear-to-ear as he packed her groceries inside two brown paper bags. She returned the magazine to its rack and brushed her hair away from her face. Shot a seductive glance at Danny and then turned her glance at Don Pepe.

"Oiga, señor. Danny is growing up to be un papi chulo. You better be careful. Soon the girls will be knocking down the door going after him. Hey Danny, do you have a girlfriend?" Elena asked, enjoying the sight of Danny blushing.

He shook his head and buried himself inside the biology book. He felt uneasy having Elena there talking to him. One thing was to watch her from a distance, another was to have a conversation with her. Having his father standing a few feet away added to the embarrassment.

Freddy saw the discomfort on Danny's flustered face and quickly approached the counter. Elena switched her eyes at him, her mischievous grin increasing the depth of her dimples. Don Pepe went behind the counter and began preparing a sandwich on two slices of white bread.

They all watched him, like keen observers, as he smeared mayonnaise on one slice, mustard on the other. He added ham, olive loaf, bologna, American cheese, a few leaves of lettuce and two slices of tomatoes. Sprinkled pepper and salt. He placed the sandwich on a plate, sliced it in half and adorned it with two pickles. "Here Freddy," he said, pushing the plate to the front of the counter. "Take a soda or a juice if you want."

"Muchas gracias, señor," Freddy said, thanking him as he stuck half his body inside the large refrigerator filled with soda, juice, bottled water and beer.

"That looks good," Elena said, admiring the overstuffed sandwich.

"Do you want one?" Don Pepe asked, wrapping the cold cuts. "I'll make you one, too. It's on the house."

"No it's okay. Thanks anyway. I already made dinner and lately I've been putting a few extra pounds on that I don't need. Estoy gorda," Elena said, patting her flat stomach pretending it was fat. A thought not shared by the men. "And Johnny should be home soon, the rare times that he comes early."

"I haven't seen your husband in a long time," Don Pepe said, putting the cold cuts away. "That man is like a ghost."

"Even the twins are complaining about it," she said. Then she stiffened and yawned. "I understand that he wants a better life for us, and his big dream is to buy a house and get out of this neighborhood. But, what's the sense of working so hard for a family that's becoming strangers to you?"

"Maybe he should cut down a few hours," Don Pepe said, noticing the seriousness in Elena's eyes. She no longer looked so young and pretty. She resembled the typical housewife that was not content with a life that was passing her by. It brought memories of his own Sophy before she became used to his slave-like hours at the bodega. There were times when a man must take action in order to be a good provider, even if those actions were not agreeable by everyone involved. You couldn't keep the cow just for milk, there would be a time when you'd rather have a steak, and killing the cow was inevitable.

"Cut hours?" Elena tried to regain her peppiness, although her shield had been cracked. "He is committed to his jobs. Even on his days off from one job, he finds a way to work overtime at the other one. I'm beginning to wonder if the real reason is me. What can I do Don Pepe? I'm tired of bitchin' about it. Whenever it's convenient for him, he suddenly becomes deaf. Only his mother gets his attention. If he keeps that up, I'll tell you, he could stay with his mother and I'll leave. I'm still young and pretty. I shouldn't have a problem getting myself another man. Right, Freddy?"

Freddy nodded between bites. Like almost every man on the block, he had fantasized about Elena in different ways. And he had a few things to his advantage. He was single, young and knew of lots of places where he could take a woman, where she could get all dressed up and feel like a queen. Freddy could feel Don Pepe's harsh glare.

Was the old man jealous? Nah. Just looking after him like always. Ever since both of his parents had left for Puerto Rico (while he stayed to pursue his music career), Don Pepe had taken him under his wings. He'd always made sure that Freddy was eating right and a few times had helped him pay his rent. The man was a saint and Freddy could not wait to make it big and repay Don Pepe for all his unselfish kindness.

Manolo finished packing Elena's groceries and Don Pepe had never seen the young man bag groceries so slowly. Perhaps the slight cleavage peeking lustfully through Elena's blouse was the cause of the slowness in Manolo's hands. Don Pepe was surrounded by a bunch of young men who were reacting to the woman inside the store, the Cleopatra of El Barrio. Even his son was learning more about biology with her than with the information in the textbook. To be young, single and with unused hormones rushing through your bod, like wild stallions in open fields of the Wild West.

"Elena!" a man called out from outside. It was her husband, Johnny. He rushed forward and stood in front of the door with no desire to enter. His tired eyes swept inside and landed angrily upon Elena. A sneer twitched the right side of his upper lip.

"Hello, Johnny. ¿Qué dice el hombre?" Don Pepe asked, greeting the upset man, hoping to defuse an ugly situation before it started. There were rumors that Johnny had quick hands when dealing with his wife. "Haven't seen you in a long time. Stop in once in a while and say hello."

Johnny's tensed stare shot up to Don Pepe. His sneering lip twitched a bit faster. His beady eyes locked with Manolo's, until the young grocer looked with faked interest at Danny's schoolwork. Johnny's head turned slightly and his bullish glare found Freddy. He looked at the musician with hateful eyes.

Freddy took a few bold steps forward. His body language inviting Johnny to take his best shot. Primitive machismo minds visiting the wildness of the beginning of time. Johnny twirled away from Freddy and his abashed eyes fell accusingly on Elena. Freddy's lips curled upward in a victorious smile. Just one stare-down, exposed Johnny as what he truly was. A momma's boy.

A big stupid tough guy with the ladies only. Shrinking at the sight of a man that could sweep the whole neighborhood with his sorry ass. This made Freddy want Elena even more. Not so much for her love or lustful body, but to ridicule her asshole husband. Pleasure could be spelled many different ways.

"Did you buy any Yoo-hoos?" Johnny asked his wife. His voice a pathetic yelp, from a pathetic man. "If you're wasting your time here, you may as well buy something I want."

"What do you mean wasting my time? I needed milk and Cornflakes for the boys. They have to eat something for breakfast tomorrow."

"Didn't you buy milk and a box of cereal yesterday?"

"Yes, I did! But your mother finished everything and waited after I had cooked dinner to tell me. Otherwise I would have bought what I needed on my way from picking up the twins."

Johnny scowled at Elena's burning eyes.

Someone is going to sleep hurting tonight, Johnny thought in his twisted mind. The men around them pretended there were other things to occupy their interest, except for Freddy. He leaned on a shelf, where boxes of cat food were neatly stacked and didn't hide his amusement.

Freddy wanted a piece of Johnny. He wanted it bad. He could taste it. Johnny rushed by him to get his Yoo-hoos. His face a dark shade of embarrassment, plain imbecilic anger. Freddy caught Elena's face and winked at her in defiance. She winked back and shrugged her shoulders playfully. Don Pepe's stern and serious frown disapproved of their childish behavior. Danny enjoyed the sideshow and Manolo wished he was as cool and as nonchalant as Freddy. No wonder the man wore dark shades in the night.

Johnny came back, holding two six-packs of Yoo-hoos and a box of Oreos under his arm. He looked like a spoiled brat stacking up with goodies to devour by himself while watching *Star Trek*. He shoved his items on top of the counter and removed his wallet from his back pocket.

Manolo packed the chocolate drinks and cookies. The thick tension hung on the air like a cold winter morning fog. Danny's flipping of his textbook snapped crisp and loud. Elena's perfume overpowering the staleness of the bodega. Freddy wrapped his shades around his eyes, looking like a hitman ready to snuff a doomed victim.

Don Pepe went to the register and began rummaging through slips and receipts that had accumulated. The radio blared a silky and slow Tito

Rodríguez bolero about the loneliness shared by two solitary beings.

Elena and Johnny took their groceries and threw themselves into the night. No one but them would now how it would end. The bodega took on an eeriness that belittled those that had entered and those that would exit. Danny closed his book and knew that tomorrow's test was going to be another excellent mark in his school's records. Manolo removed the apron he had purchased with his money, just to feel more important, more in charge than the neighborhood patrons. Freddy squinted at the night through eyes darker than the shadows that engulfed him. Don Pepe acknowledged the twilight of a day that had ended the same way it had started, with no false promises of what awaited beyond.

The dimly-lit bars began to gather troublemakers, dealers and junkies. Hardworking men with no place to go and others who did have a place to go. That felt that a stool and a few cold ones were better than a wife, kids and hypnotizing television light.

The phone rang, smashing the silence of the bodega. It rang twice before Don Pepe stuck the receiver to his ear. He grinned and groaned a few times. Threw a couple of yeses and with a slight smile hung up. "Hey Danny, that was your mother. She figured that you'd forget the things she told you to bring home. You forgot...right?"

"Forgot what?"

"Just like she thought, you forgot. Get some milk, toilet paper and a box of crackers," Don Pepe said, turning to Manolo. "Is Miguel picking you up tonight? Because if he's not, you should leave before it gets any later. You have a long way to go. By the way, you didn't have any classes tonight?"

"No, the classes were cancelled for the whole week. The teacher had a death in the family. And I think that Miguel had a few things to do, so I'm not going to wait for him. I guess I should start my trip back home. I'll see you tomorrow, Don Pepe. Buenas noches. Hey, Danny...hey Freddy...hasta mañana."

"Freddy, can I see you for a second?" Don Pepe asked, nodding to Freddy and motioning him to meet outside.

Freddy followed, watching Don Pepe's broad shoulders. The night was cool and comfortable. A big round moon weaved through nocturnal clouds. Don Pepe inhaled at the aroma of fried food coming from the cuchifrito place across the street. He put his arm around Freddy's shoulders like a supportive father looking out for the wellbeing of a son. "I hope you don't mind me telling you this, but remember one thing. I just want the best for you. You are like a son to me, and if I'm out of line I'll respect your wishes if you tell me to mind my own business."

"Please, señor. I will never tell you that. If you see something that I'm doing wrong, feel free to tell me. Even if I agree or not, you will never be out of line in my book."

"Bueno hijo, gracias. But what are you doing? I couldn't help notice the little game playing with the eyes between you and Elena. She's a married woman with two big responsibilities on her hands. Look around you, there are more fish in the ocean. Why do you want to steal a fish from the basket of another man when the waters are full with others ready to jump in your basket? That woman, my son, is forbidden fruit. I don't know if what she's doing, she is doing it on purpose, and actually I don't care. What I do care about is not seeing someone that I consider a son putting himself in a position that could lead to bigtime trouble. You don't need that."

"I know, señor...but her husband is an asshole."

"He could be an asshole, but you know what? That's her problem, not yours. That asshole is supporting her, their kids and his mother. So asshole or no asshole, the bottom line is that he is there. Could you support Elena and her children?"

"Well, not really."

"No, not really nothing. The answer is no. Besides if you could, why get involved in the life of a married woman?"

"Because she's not happy in that marriage."

"How do you know that? And even if she's not, would you be able to make her happier?"

"Sure I can."

"Freddy, I don't mean just in bed. I mean the whole nine yards. Not just becoming her lover, but becoming her man and provider. Could you do that? On the salary of a struggling musician?"

Freddy was at a loss for words. His shaded eyes glanced at the distance. Like looking through a magical door that revealed a bit of a taste of what the future was willing to give you and what you were willing to get. Don Pepe was right. Like always. No wonder he had raised three wonderful children that not only cared for one another, but also cared for him with the same unselfish enthusiasm.

Why hadn't God made Don Pepe his father, too? Well at least God did the second best thing. He made Don Pepe his friend and father figure all rolled into one package of love. Freddy put Don Pepe on a pedestal that not even his own father had ever stood on.

"Mira, Freddy," Don Pepe said, squeezing the young man's arm. "I'm not here to preach to you or try to come out as if I have all the answers, because I do not. I'm just trying to throw a few pennies inside your wishing well to make you understand that sometimes a little splash could easily turn into a tidal wave of destruction. You're a good kid with dreams. It's going to take a lot of sacrifices in order for you to make it, then again you may not. But you cannot shoot yourself in the foot before the battle begins. Elena is a teaser. We all know that. She's a sweet young lady, but her eyes are always roaming to the next guy in line. You don't need that. And definitely, you don't need a jealous husband trying to make himself bigger than he truly is by putting a bullet between your eyes. For what? Because you're chasing a woman's wink. An empty wink with nothing to offer you but plain trouble. There are finer women out there waiting for someone like you. Why go after somebody's leftovers, when there's a fresh dish waiting for you on your own table?"

Freddy removed the dark glasses and hugged Don Pepe. "I'm very lucky to be around someone like you. No wonder your children turned out the way they did. You should write a book about fatherhood."

"Are you crazy? That's the reason this world is such a mess. Too many people writing books and claiming to be experts, when all they're doing is confusing everyone. Just listen to your heart and the good life will follow. Besides, I didn't do this by myself. Sophy was the anchor in our lives. She is more responsible than me. I'll give her all the credit." Don Pepe let go of Freddy and rocked himself on his heels. He raised his left wrist to his eyes and was surprised that it was almost ten-thirty. "At what time is this showcase? By the time you get to Astoria, it's going to be awfully late."

"Actually," Freddy said, clearing his throat. "The showcase is tomorrow. I just didn't want to tell Elena that the real reason that I'm all dressed up is because I have a date."

Don Pepe snickered and stretched his neck sideways. "Now, why did you do that? Were you afraid that Elena was going to get jealous?"

"I know that it sounds stupid. But yes, I didn't want her to find out. It's stupid, right?"

"You know the answer for that, hijo. Anyway, go out and enjoy yourself on this secret date. But be careful and I don't mean just out in the street," Don Pepe said, winking and slapping Freddy's back.

"I'll be careful, señor. Thanks again. Buenas noches, I'll see you soon."

"Buenas noches, hijo. Que Dios te bendiga." Don Pepe watched as Freddy hid his face behind his shades and started walking toward the train station. His black silhouette camouflaged in the dark street.

From inside the bodega Danny had gathered the groceries his mother asked for, plus a few extra goodies for himself. His books were packed inside his schoolbag as he viewed the last innings of the Yankees game. He pried his eyes from the small screen and looked toward the sidewalk. Freddy had just left and his father, like a mayor from a small town seeking votes, waved and smiled at the passersby. It was amazing how much his father was respected by everyone in the neighborhood. Regardless if they were the meekest or toughest.

Even the cutthroat drug dealers nodded courteously as they went by. His father greeted everyone the same. With sincerity and genuine hospitality. He stood underneath a lamppost, its lazy yellow light falling on him like a spotlight. His thin gray hair escaping under his weathered Yankees cap. His father seemed much older now than ever. Danny felt a certain sadness at this revelation and wished he could stop time now. So that this day, this era in his life, would never end.

Don Pepe came inside, wrinkles on his face more pronounced than Danny had ever remembered seeing. His once strong broad shoulders sagged with less strength under his shirt. "Is the game over?" Don Pepe asked, as he took a chip from the open bag on the counter. The sourness crinkled his face as he swallowed. "What are you eating, son?"

"Salt and vinegar chips," Danny said, tilting his head and stuffing his mouth.

"They forgot the salt and overdid it with the vinegar, if you ask me."

"Come on dad, you have to get used to the taste."

"Son, that will kill your taste buds forever. What's wrong? You don't like Cheez Doodles? I still sell them."

"Yeah dad, but to who? The little kids that don't know any better? Or to the old people that hate to change?"

"Are you calling me old just because I like Cheez Doodles?"

"No, I'm not calling you old. I'm just saying that Cheez Doodles are boring," Danny said, his eyes twinkling with laughter.

"Boring?" Don Pepe's eyebrows arched sharply. "Since when does a simple snack become boring? How do you describe that awful stuff that you're eating?"

"They're cool."

"If you say so, son. I'll stick to my boring Cheez Doodles if you don't mind."

Danny rolled his eyes playfully and turned the television off, but not before getting a glimpse of a reporter with Grand Central Terminal as back scenery. It was the coming lead story after the game. The story that had exploded all over New York City.

"Hey dad…that man that shot himself. You knew him, right?"

"Yes, I did." Don Pepe removed his hat and dragged his fingers through his thinning hair. "As I was telling Freddy, I saw that kid grow up. Thank God his parents are already dead, otherwise this would've killed them."

Danny noticed the anguish in his father's eyes. "Tito mentioned something about seeing the guy early this morning and that the man was just staring at the building where he used to live. Did you see him?"

"No. I'm sorry that I didn't. I wonder that if I did, would I have been able to make a difference?"

"Maybe not. He probably had made up his mind."

"Well, there are times that even if your mind is made up, it could easily be changed if you really want to. Nothing is carved in stone."

"Was he a junkie, like Jimmy?"

"I don't know. All I know is that he had more problems than anyone realized. Ever since he got shot when he was a little boy, he was never the same. Even though he moved away from the neighborhood, once in a while he popped around. Usually he would spend time with Jimmy, but most of the time he was alone.

Maybe that was his real killer. The mad ghosts that fill your head with nonsense whenever too much time is spent alone. Man was not meant to be by himself, that's why God created Eve."

"Why can't the cops or somebody do something about all the drugs? Is it possible?"

"Well son, your old man has been around for a few years. And I'll tell you, drugs existed even back when I was young. It's a very profitable epidemic. Too many people are getting rich because of the weakness of others. I don't mean just the pushers out on the streets. Those are actually small potatoes when you compare them with the rich businessmen with their fancy mansions and chauffeured limos. Too much green to go unnoticed. Too much green that easily corrupts the mind of anyone with no backbone. From top politicians and Wall Street executives down to the lowlife on the corner. You want to get high son, get high on the fumes of printed words in books. Get high on the knowledge that will feed your hungry brain. Never waste yourself nor your future with the junk that's out there poisoning people. I know that there's always that peer pressure. But always remember that there is no such thing as peer pressure when you are a leader. Peer pressure is only concerned with the followers that will never accomplish anything in their sorry lives."

Danny crumbled the empty bag of chips into a ball and deposited it inside a trashcan behind him. His father's moistened eyes faded under the shadows of his cap. He could tell his father was upset about the man's death. That was his dad, always feeling the pains of others. Realizing the disturbance which the whole event had taken on him, Danny changed the subject to something more wholesome and fresh, away the ugliness of the real world. "By the way dad, the Yankees won in the last inning. They came back after losing by four runs."

"Who was pitching today?" Don Pepe asked, stretching his back and lifting his arms like a holdup victim.

"Andy Pettitte started the game, but Edgar Martinez hit two homeruns. He got five RBIs with those two swings."

"Who started for Seattle?"

"Randy Johnson. Boy was he tough! Thank God for the Mariners' bullpen. The Yankees were able to jump ahead. Paul O'Neill and Tino Martinez hit back-to-back homeruns. Bernie Williams kept the inning alive and Derek Jeter came up with the winning run. The Yankees sent ten batters to the plate that inning. You missed a good game."

"The season just began. Hopefully there should be more games like that before October comes around."

"Do you think that they have a chance at winning the World Series?"

"Anything's possible. But you still have a lot of great teams in the American League. And let's not forget the Braves in the National League. We'll see where we stand come fall."

"We have to get tickets for some of the games, maybe we could take Manolo. Do you believe that he's never been to a game?"

"Yes, I believe it. I think that it will be a good idea, I'm pretty sure that he'll like that. Well son, are you ready? I'm tired and it's time to go home."

"I was ready a long time ago. I already packed the things that mom wanted and if you don't mind, I took a few extra for myself."

"Let me guess. Salt and vinegar chips?"

Danny laughed as he came down on his feet from the stool behind the counter. He strolled around, flung his schoolbag over his shoulder, and squeezed the bag of groceries onto his chest. He yawned widely and went outside.

Somewhere hidden by the shadows and the continuous flow of cars, Danny heard a whining alarm from a car. Young thugs, as young as him and even younger, stared at him with cold street-educated eyes. A slow-moving patrol car scanned the area just to make its presence felt. From above the store, loud Spanish soap operas spilled out laughable dialogue of love and hate.

The corner bar's red blinking lights invited those with money to enter its domain. Fat old women argued and wondered whatever happened to their long lost beauty and sultry curves while munching on fried food from the cuchifrito. Dogs barked and growled in empty littered lots. Danny turned as the lights from the bodega went off. The sidewalk took a menacingly lonely look. He waited for his father to come out and his anxieties grew with a hint of fear.

This was the hour he hated spending time at the store. At closing time. When robbers knew that the last one out had money weighing down their pockets. Too many desperate souls, which for a few bucks to carry them from night to morning, would go through extreme measures to fulfill that deadly drive. Danny looked around, searching the dark for telltale signs of a strung-out predator seeking a quick unearned payday.

Don Pepe pulled the gate down until it met the concrete. He slipped and locked the two heavy-duty locks and shook them to assure himself that his store was well protected. He gazed at Danny and couldn't help but notice how vulnerable and out of place his son looked. A few more years, and if God permits, Danny would go to college and away from all this negative garbage that surrounded them.

And only then, would Don Pepe be able to sell the store and retire peacefully. Someplace where cars don't sound like nightclubs on wheels. Where no shady characters snatched the streets from hardworking souls searching for a better life. Someplace where life could be accepted and cherished the way God meant it to be. With love and peace.

Don Pepe had sacrificed himself for the wellbeing and future of his children, and thanks to God and the Holy Virgin Mary, he was approaching the threshold of that fabled land. Don Pepe smiled at his handsome son and wrapped his arm around him. They walked through the dark streets of Spanish Harlem as one.

"What is your mother making for dinner?"

Danny shifted his shoulder to accommodate his knapsack as Don Pepe took the bag of groceries from him. "I think that she's making steak with onions and yellow rice."

"Qué bueno, bistec con cebolla y arroz. My favorite," Don Pepe said, licking his lips with mouthwatering anticipation.

"I know, I like that too. I can't wait to dip my salt and vinegar chips in the meat gravy."

"Please son, why ruin something so delicious?"

"Yeh dad, you're right. I should just have the chips dry. Why ruin them?"

Don Pepe squeezed his son with an embrace laced with love. "Where did I go wrong with you?"

"I don't know, dad. Maybe from the time that you made me a Yankees fan. Who knows, I was probably a Mets fan."

"Over my dead body you'll be a Mets fan. Over my dead body."

They laughed as they walked happily among the broken lives and cursed out dreams that loomed around them. Don Pepe glanced back at the bodega. His mistress, the only woman other than his wife that he bowed to. The only woman who beheld him in a stronghold that was unbreakable and untouched.

He was going now to his wife, to his life, to the reason for waking up every morning and pushing himself to the maximum madness of destruction. He was a provider and therefore he had to provide, regardless if his body and soul wanted to hear another song on the radio before getting up in the morning.

Just another song that could easily turn into two songs, or three, or even a few hours' worth of music. He was the slave and the master in a society which claimed that no such things existed. Someday he would bask under the golden soothing sunshine of Puerto Rico or the caresses of a simple picnic in Central Park.

It would come like a well-deserved reunion with a past and present that would dictate a beautiful tomorrow. A reunion where you wouldn't need a tag that spelled your name, nor be forced to lie about who you were and who you weren't. Don Pepe waved when someone from across the street shouted his name, continuing on the familiar march with his son. He began to whistle as his arm tightened around Danny's shoulder.

Tomorrow would be another glorious day willing to share its tales and laughter. He rushed along as his happy out-of-tune whistling played on. Again, out of habit.

"UNDER THE HOOD"

(Based on a short story by Mary Lofaro)

ONE

Robert rolled over in bed and landed on his ass. The hard slam on the wooden floor woke him up fast. He looked up, blinking stupidly as if expecting someone to peek out from above the bed and yell *'gotcha'!* He was still wearing the same clothes he wore two days ago and his stench was offensive, even for him. He sat up and squinted. A forty-ounce beer lay on its side, half its contents had spilled onto the bare mattress, staining the fabric in a dark blotch.

He got on his knees, reached for the bottle, and sat back down on the floor to tilt his head back and wash the slimy taste in his mouth with the last bit of warm beer inside. His body jerked slightly as the alcohol awoke his nasty hangover, making his stomach rumble with a washout discomfort.

He got on his feet and his legs wobbled as if he were standing on a moving platform. He closed his eyes and took a deep breath and with his eyes half closed he shuffled to the bathroom. He stepped inside the bathtub without undressing and turned on the water. Cold water first then hot. The water hit his face and he began to undress, realizing he was still wearing his construction boots. He mumbled a curse and sat on the edge of the tub to remove them, the water splashing all over the floor.

He removed all his clothes and threw them on the soaked floor with indifference and returned to the powerful massage of the shower, as it removed layers of old sweat and the stench of alcohol. He lathered twice. Before turning off the water he stood under the shower for a few more minutes. It felt so good that he would have loved to have just stayed there for the whole day, but he couldn't. Today he was meeting Papo and if the plan went right, they were looking to make a few hundred bucks in less than ten minutes.

It was ten after six on an early Friday morning.

TWO

Kevin heard the alarm clock go on and off almost at the same moment. Without a doubt, this feat was a gift his wife had, it had to be. There was no other explanation for why a human being could shut down an alarm radio within seconds of it going off, without missing a beat. His wife enjoyed her sleep. He bet that if ever she were posed with the question of what she loved most, her husband or her sleep—she would choose sleep. And her answer would be given with the same quickness that she showed when turning the alarm radio off.

He smiled as he slipped on a freshly cleaned pair of overalls and walked down the stairs to the kitchen. If there was a contest for the cleanest, best smelling car mechanic in the world, he would win the prize hands down. His wife, Meg, was the type of person you had to always be looking your best for. There was nothing she loved more than clean smelling things. Damn, he thought, he was lucky that she allowed him to even enter the house after a hard day's work, when every inch of his body was covered with grease and grime.

He grabbed the coffeepot and poured water down the coffee maker's reservoir. He took a filter from the fridge and scooped two heaping spoons of coffee, returned the pot to its holder and turned the coffee on. By the time she'd wake up in half an hour the coffee would be hot and strong, or as she jokingly said once, "just the way I like my men." He gathered his wallet, keys and pens and climbed up the stairs to the bedroom.

He could hear the soft snores coming from her, the floral quilt raising ever so slowly around her body. He leaned forward and swept his lips gently on his wife's forehead. Her hair smelled wonderful and he wished it were a holiday so he could slip next to her and hold her in his arms until noon. He looked down at her lovely face and his love for her grew greater. Kevin and

Meg had been married for eight wonderful years and their relationship kept growing stronger, deeper, and he knew that this was the woman he wanted to be with until life stood still.

The first time they had met, it was not only her beauty, but also her intelligence that floored him as if he had been stung by a sucker punch. She reveled in the simplicity of life and the way she approached it was with ease and determination. It was as if she knew that God had given her a gift, a priceless one, and there was nothing she would ever do to tarnish it. Their conversations were endless hours of laughter and deeply moving emotions. A single phrase would spawn hours of being mesmerized by the magic of each other's company and thoughts.

They did debate on subjects where their opinions differed, but like educated, civilized scholars they would present each other's arguments without quarrels or cross-eyed anger. Except of course when it came to baseball. She was a devoted Mets fan and he in turn bled Yankees' pinstripes. But even that they settled diplomatically; one day of the year he was forced to go to a Mets game wearing a Mets cap and in return she attended a Yankees game with Yankee headgear. He leaned and kissed her again, this time tasting the fullness of her lips.

"I love you sweetheart," Kevin whispered and kissed her again. Meg smiled and uttered something unintelligible as he slapped her bottom playfully and left the room, closing the door behind him.

He climbed inside his car and turned on the ignition, the car roaring like a well-trained tiger. He pulled out of the driveway and onto the quiet streets of his neighborhood. He pointed the car toward the highway and turned on the radio to the classic rock and roll station. It was a beautiful day, and as he drove happily through the still sleepy streets he decided there and then that he was going to call Meg and plan a great night that would begin in their favorite Italian restaurant and would end in the softness of her arms.

Yes, Kevin smiled as he sang along with Billy Joel, *"I love you just the way you are"*. It was ten after six on an early Friday morning.

THREE

Papo swung his feet from the bed and slammed them hard against the linoleum floor. "*Puñeta!*" he screamed and spat on the floor with disgust. "What the fuck? Don't ya' hear the kid cryin'?"

"Don't youse start with me now, shit," Millie said, her voice muffled by the pillow. "You got the same right to take care of him, youse his father too, *cabrón*."

Papo stared at Millie and then across the bedroom where the crib was pushed against the wall. Their son was almost one year old, but damn did the boy have a pair of lungs. He was probably wet from head to toe, his little belly aching with hunger. Wouldn't it be nice to be a baby again, Papo thought, when everybody did things for you. All you had to do was start a big mess and there was someone taking care of your needs.

He stood up and walked to the crib and looked down. His little face was red and soaked with tears as Papo lifted him carefully and folded him into his chest. He felt the tiny body trembling and Papo kissed the little boy's face, hoping to stop his crying. The wailing subdued a bit and that made Papo smile.

"Damn boy, you're wet," he whispered in his son's ear, as he bounced him gently on his shoulder.

He scooped a diaper from the box and took the baby to the bed. "Hey Millie, don't let him fall. I'm gonna get the powder." He took two steps and stared at Millie. "Yo' girl, I'm talkin' to you. Ain't you up?"

"Jesus!" Millie said, raising her head, shooting an angry look at Papo. "Why is it that all goddamn day I have to take care of him by myself and you can't even change his fuckin' diaper without a fuckin' audience?"

"Someone woke up on the wrong side of the bed."

"No motherfucker. Nobody here woke up from no wrong side of the bed. It's youse that woke my ass up the wrong fuckin' way."

Papo wanted to yell at her, but decided it was best to just take care of Lil' Tony and ignored her. She was crankier than ever lately. Everything bothered her and all she wanted to do was hang out with friends day and night. He knew she hated being a mother, but damn things happen and the little boy was helpless and needed care and love from both of them. Poor kid didn't choose to be born, but it seemed that Millie became more distant every day, angrier as if she wanted nothing to do with the child.

Papo went into the living room and found the powder on top of the small kitchenette table, hurried back to the bedroom. He was glad he did. Millie had gone back to sleep and Lil' Tony was a few inches from falling off the bed. Papo grabbed the kid by his leg and positioned him on the bed to remove the soaked diaper, after cleaning him with a damp towel and sprinkling some powder. Slipped the clean dry diaper on. The t-shirt was also wet and Papo changed that, too. With that the baby let out a string of gibberish, as if telling Papo how grateful he was.

He lifted the baby and gently rocked him, enjoying how his son smelled. One thing that always amazed him was how babies never had bad breath and they had a sweet and pleasant scent that seeped through their pores, like the way angels might smell. He left the bedroom and Millie's foul mood and went to the small kitchen and opened the refrigerator door, took the bottle of premixed formula and placed it inside a pot filled halfway with water. Heated it up.

He remembered the first time Lil' Tony was born and how he was afraid to hold him. Lil' Tony had looked so fragile, so tiny that the thought of accidentally squeezing the baby to death ran through his mind. But then something magical happened. The kid was strong and his softness was not as soft as it looked. There was a bond he developed with his son and it was an enchanting experience only shared by them. Something that was lacking between his son and Millie. She'd had a pregnancy that could be described as bitchy.

Everything under the sun bothered her. She complained about the weight she'd gained and the baggy, tent-like clothes. She was angry because she couldn't hang out with her friends as often as she wanted to, especially when the delivery date neared.

Papo removed the bottle from the pot and shook a few drops of the milk on his wrist to make sure it wasn't too hot for Lil' Tony. He turned off the stove and shuffled to the living room and sat down on the worn-out couch. He felt his body sink deep inside the wasted cushions. He held the baby on the fold of his arm, supported by his chest and placed the nipple inside the awaiting lips. The kid was so hungry he sucked with great force and soon a whistling sound rang out.

"This crazy life is not for you," Papo whispered to his son. "No boy of mine is gonna live like a damn pig. You're gonna be somebody, you hear me kid? You're gonna grow up to be the fuckin' President of the goddamn United States. Yep, you know what I mean? You gonna be the first Puerto Rican to enter the White House through the front door. No service entrances for you, my boy. You gonna be somebody bigger than any motherfucker out there."

Lil' Tony spit out some milk from the side of his mouth, took a second rest and started sucking again, his alert brown eyes shining like old-fashioned marbles.

"Your mom don't love you," Papo said, kissing the baby's forehead. "But it's okay. We don't need the bitch. We are men; we are fuckin' survivors. You'll see Lil' Tony. After today we are both out of here. No more nasty bitch snoring like a pig when my little boy is crying of hunger. I'll always be here for you boy, know what I mean? I'll always be here for you. Daddy ain't gonna let his Kung-Fu baby boy down."

Papo removed the empty bottle from Lil' Tony's lips and placed it on the table in front of him. He cuddled the satisfied child as the early morning sun framed them in a perfect family shot. As the day began to awaken, Papo and Lil' Tony took a nap and it would be the last time father and son would love each other.

It was ten after six on an early Friday morning.

FOUR

Ryan opened his eyes and glared at the ringing alarm clock. He stared at the annoying apparatus as if wondering how the hell it got there in the first place. His wife Karen shifted away from the shrieking sound and squeezed the pillow tight around her head.

"Come on, could you turn that off?" she mumbled, with a voice lacking strength.

Ryan reached out and turned the alarm off, almost hitting the snooze button, but deciding against it at the last second. Today his daughter Allison was going on a school trip and to give his wife a break, he volunteered to drive her early on his way to the garage. Besides, Allison loved going to the garage, there was a tomboy streak in her, not like her younger sister Tess that favored everything pink and delicate.

Allison loved the feel of his tools on her hands and she adored going to the garage as often as possible, just to have the chance to turn a bolt or remove a spark plug from a car being overhauled. She loved to be around her Uncle Kevin. Ryan's brother was a pushover when it came to his nieces. There wasn't anything in the world he wouldn't do for them. On their birthdays and Christmas, he backed up his pickup truck into the loading dock of Toys R Us and just emptied the whole aisle of girl's stuff it seemed!

Allison was also a big Yankees fan, just like Kevin, and they would spend hours talking trivia about the boys of summer. Ryan was convinced that Allison knew more Yankee history than the Baseball Hall of Fame.

Ryan slipped out from under the covers and touched the shaggy rug with his bare feet. He dug his toes into the thick rug; it was something he began doing after watching Bruce Willis do it in the first "Die Hard" movie. Maybe it was just in his mind, but just like the movie it was relaxing and he felt it was the best way to begin the day. His own form of meditation, Hollywood-make-believe style.

He stretched his arms over his head, crunching his shoulder blades as far as they could go and inhaled, raising his ribs and sucking in his stomach. He did this at least ten times and then he got up, passing his hand over his stomach and noticing that the few beers he'd drank during the week were beginning to find a permanent home in his belly.

He staggered to the bathroom, and as he passed the girl's room, Allison swung the door open. He wasn't surprised. She was already dressed, her peppy mood bouncing around like some rubber ball gone haywire. She jumped on his neck and kissed him. Ryan held his breath, not wanting to give her a dose of his morning stench. She didn't seem to care and was a happy child.

"Morning, dad," Allison greeted cheerfully.

Ryan mumbled a return greeting as he stepped inside the bathroom and closed the door. Now he was able to talk freely. "Honey, give me a half hour and we'll be on our way."

"Okay dad," Allison said from the other side of the door. "I'll have some cereal while you get ready."

"That's my girl," Ryan said, as he turned the water on in the sink and took a piss. He undressed and took a look at himself in the mirror. He twisted his face from side to side and lifted his chin to peek underneath. It was a ritual he did every morning to decide if he could go another day without shaving. He hated to shave. Maybe he should grow a beard, he thought. A beard, the idea took life.

It would make him look distinguished, he tried to convince himself, intelligent like some college professor. Karen would hate it. He knew his wife was not fond of facial hair. She might get used to the idea and he tried to justify his reasons for growing a beard. Then again she might refuse to kiss me, he contemplated. He lathered his face and took out a new disposable razor and killed the beard before it had a chance to grow.

Ryan came down feeling clean and fresh and found Allison slouched on the couch watching television. "Good morning sweetheart," he said, going

126

over to his daughter. He kissed her with confidence. The difference toothpaste and mouthwash does to the way you say hello. "What are you watching?"

"Sportscenter," Allison answered, as she leaned forward to the edge of the couch. Her eyes were glued to the screen without blinking. They were about to start with Yankees highlights from last night's ballgame. Even though she had watched the game and stayed awake until the postgame report, she couldn't get enough. Ryan knew the Yankees had won the game, otherwise she would've turned the television off the second she had seen the highlights. She hated when they lost.

Ryan scooped up his everyday essentials, a Timex watch, keys and two Bic pens, which he always deposited in the same spot every night after work; an ashtray he had molded way back in junior high school during an arts and crafts class. It was a monstrosity of misshapen brown ceramic, but it held sentimental value for him. The teacher that instructed the class was a young sexy blonde that looked very much like Debbie Harry from the punk band Blondie, and every guy — and most likely every male teacher — had a crush on her.

She had helped him in shaping the clay into something that resembled an ashtray. Her hair had brushed against his cheek and it felt silky. To this day he could still remember that it smelled like cherries. Her slender fingers had wrapped around his clumsy, sweaty hands guiding him to sculpt the lump of clay into something recognizable, but little did she know that she was also helping him reshape something else.

That day he had felt special and every time he looked at the ashtray it rekindled that first moment of adolescent lust. When Karen tried to throw it out he pretended that a best friend from school had made it a few days before being run over by a car and killed instantly. She had believed him until Kevin got a whiff of the story and destroyed the myth of the tragic tale by revealing its true sentimental value.

Between hysterical laughs from everyone and a lot of ribbing from Karen, Kevin roaring in laughter told the real story of the ashtray or as he had plainly phrased it: "That was Ryan's private way of popping his virginal cherry in his mind."

Ryan chuckled and received a strange stare from Allison. As he grabbed the doorknob, Karen came down, her eyes still swollen with sleep. "Allison," she said, rubbing her eyes and letting out a yawn. "Don't forget to take a sweater with you, it's a bit chilly now and definitely is going to be chilly later on."

"Oh mom, it's April," Allison protested. It was something she started doing lately, behaving like any other kid reaching the preteen threshold, the age of rebellion.

"I know it's April and it's only fifty-two degrees outside. This evening it's supposed to drop down to the forties, maybe even colder."

Allison went up the stairs pretending to be upset, more preteen angst.

Ryan came from behind and wrapped his arms around Karen's waist. She felt soft and warm, like a comfortable quilt in the middle of a cold winter night. He kissed the back of her neck. "That girl has your temperament," he said smiling.

"And don't forget my good looks too," Karen said, flapping her eyelids seductively. Then she laughed as she twirled her body to face Ryan. She locked her arms around his neck and kissed him hard on his lips. "What do you think buster, do I still have it?" she asked, oozing sexuality.

Ryan kissed her lips and smirked. "Still the same vamp that switched tables at Patrick's wedding just so you could sit at mine."

They laughed and held each other like young lovers meeting after being separated for a long time. They had met at the wedding of a mutual friend and when Ryan saw her across the room his heart stopped. She was a gorgeous woman with curly red hair that fell on her shoulders. She carried herself with confidence and her assertiveness challenged anything that may have been an obstacle.

And to Karen, Ryan looked like a scared choirboy ready to serve the Pope at the Vatican. From that day on she knew it was love at first sight. They had chit-chatted for a while and the second she realized he was sitting at table six she became frantic knowing that her seating arrangement had placed her at table nine. So what was a woman to do in such a desperate situation after meeting the man that made her see stars?

She turned her placement card upside down and flashed it at him while faking a coincidental surprised look. "Well, what do you know? We're sitting at the same table."

She held the card by placing her fingers over her name so he wouldn't see it was written upside down. A year later they were married and every day since had been bliss.

Allison came down dragging a sweater behind her and Ryan looked up and saw that in a few years she was going to blossom into a Karen lookalike. Come to think of it, Ryan realized, both Allison and Tess came out with his wife's good looks. And that meant that little horny boys would be parading through his door soon, that for each visit he would either gain a few white hairs or lose them. Making him wonder that in a few years he would either have a full head of white or a very shiny bowling ball for a head. He shivered at the thought.

"I'll see you later honey," he said to Karen, as he kissed her goodbye and stepped out of the house. Allison right behind him. They climbed into his Pathfinder and drove off as Allison turned the radio loud to hear N'Sync screech into a predictable ballad.

It was ten after six on an early Friday morning.

FIVE

Robert swung opened the refrigerator door and looked in with disappointment shading his eyes. The coolness felt good, it reminded him when his mother used to go grocery shopping. Before going to the checkout line she used to tell him to hurry up and get some ice cream. During those times he used to stand in front of the supermarket freezer trying to decide which flavor of ice cream to take.

But now all he was sizing up were the wire shelves that held nothing but a half-empty liter bottle of Pepsi and a pack of jelly-filled cookies. His stomach rumbled and he tried to remember the last time he'd had a real meal. He closed the door and gazed around the tiny pathetic studio apartment. He walked past the front door, ignoring the second notice from the rental management office. Four months past due on his rent, and the next warning was probably going to be from the City Marshall, ready to send him a one-way ticket to homelessness.

He plopped down on one of the two cushions he'd salvaged from the garbage, when he'd moved into this dump he called home. The cushions had belonged to a decrepit thrown away couch he would've loved to have dragged into the apartment. But because he was alone at that time he had to settle for the cushions alone. When he first got the apartment he'd had steady work loading and unloading produce into trucks in Hunts Point Market up in the Bronx.

No sooner than he got the apartment he was laid off. Well, he was thrown out on his ass, something that was occurring more and more in his life. They had caught him stealing two crates of strawberries, which he was planning to sell near a subway entrance in Queens. It wasn't the first time that he'd stolen fruit from the warehouse. Just the first time most of the strawberries he stole weren't sold because of one dumb mistake.

He had tried to sell them at the Hunts Point subway station in the middle of the South Bronx; an area where not too many of the residential Puerto Ricans or Blacks bought strawberries. A buddy of his sold his stolen fruit in stations in Queens or Brooklyn, where most people were white. His buddy had told him that not too many of their people ate Cornflakes with strawberries, that was a white thing, so therefore if he wanted to get rid of the strawberries he had to travel to one of those white neighborhoods.

But Robert didn't get to find out if that theory was correct or not. They'd caught him when he'd gone to retrieve the strawberries, where he'd hid them in the garbage. That was four months ago and since then a job was a hard thing to find, especially when his skills were limited. And now of course his last place of employment was not too quick in giving him a satisfactory referral. So he was facing the ugly face of eviction. He could always go and crash for a few weeks with his mother until things get better, but his sister had taken their mother to live with her in a nice house somewhere in Queens.

Although he was always welcomed to visit, becoming a freeloader was something his sister frowned upon. A druggie freeloader, that's what he was. He leaned against the wall and came to the conclusion that he was a fuckup, a genuine Grade A, certified big time fuckup. If there were courses offered at the city college for "How to Be a Fuckup", yours truly, Mr. Robert Garcia, could be the professor.

Maybe he could even write a manual about it: "Ten Easy Steps on How to Be A Fuckup" by Robert Garcia, available in hardcover and paperback. He had to clean up his act, simple as that. How long could he go on living a life that began every day with a booster shot of negative bullshit? It's as if he were some kind of beat up car that needed to be zapped every time the ignition was clicked on.

Well, after today things were going to change.

After the job that he and Papo were going to pull off there was going to be enough money to pay the back rent and he was going to buy a nice shirt and a pair of dressy slacks. Then he was going legit. He'd apply for a job at McDonalds and take it from there. He would get a nice weekly salary, especially if he jumped at the available overtime, and he would eat for free.

He rummaged through the duffel bag where he kept clean clothes and pulled out a pair of jeans and a sweatshirt that boasted someone else's trip to Disneyland. He dug out a pair of underwear — that at one time had been white — but now were a dull beige color. He got dressed and slipped out of the apartment, stepping on the mail warning him of possible dispossession, not noticing that among the many envelopes was one with a big red lettered note from the Marshall.

When he closed the door it was eight o' clock in the morning.

SIX

Kevin parked the pickup truck in front of the garage gate. He slid out and straightened his back. The day hadn't even started and his back already felt as if angry teeth were gnawing away at it. He walked to the gate and unlocked the two heavy-duty locks, lifted the gate and yanked it all the way up—both sides riding smoothly on the greased tracks.

He went in quickly, turned off the alarm and returned to his truck and drove it inside, parking it at the spot farthest away from where all the action takes place during the day. He went upstairs to the office. It was a tiny room with no windows, but it had enough space for a small desk where he'd placed a computer and an inexpensive machine that did everything from faxing, printing and copying.

Across from the desk was an old safe that was left behind by the previous tenants. It was bulky and heavy. The thickness of the safe suggested that a nuclear bomb couldn't scratch its surface. When he and Ryan had moved into the place, they had found the safe locked and had no combination to open it. They let their imaginations run wild with the notion that perhaps there was a million dollars locked inside.

Determined to find the treasure behind the closed door, Ryan decided to play safecracker. He managed to remove the back cover of the safe and going from back to front he was able to discover the magic numbers of the combination. Kevin had been amused by the way Ryan spent hours and hours turning the dial on the front door listening attentively for any different clicking from the back. He didn't think Ryan would open the safe, but one day he began screaming like a raging lunatic:

"I did it! I did it!" Ryan came down the stairs running like a spooked man. "I opened the safe," he said, as Kevin met him at the bottom of the stairs.

"Are you going crazy?" Kevin asked.

"No man, I opened the safe. I finally got the right combination."

"Great, my brother the safecracker," Kevin said, patting him on the back. "Now if you want to play Jesse James you'll have to speed up the process. Not too many banks would be willing to give you a couple of days for you to rob them."

Ryan had either ignored or did not hear the comment. He had been too excited, almost like a child getting his first ever-solid base hit in Little League. "I didn't open the door yet. I want us to open it together."

Kevin had followed Ryan up to the office. Like a magician performing the ultimate death-defying trick, Ryan swung the door open. There was nothing inside but an empty beer bottle.

"Now we know how Geraldo Rivera felt when he sledge-hammered Al Capone's vault," Kevin said.

Both brothers looked at one another and then at the opened safe. Then back at each other. They belted out a hard satisfying laugh that rocked the entire garage.

Kevin shook his head at the memory, as he took the coffeepot that sat neatly on a table by the corner. It had been a gift from Meg to the brothers when they first opened the garage. She had called it a "garage-warming gift."

He prepared the coffee: a ritual they established and followed every morning. Have coffee and the few donuts or bagels that Ryan always brought. That was the time they talked about what was going to take place that day, which job was an emergency and which car could wait.

They spoke about their families, the sport of the season or they would sit and enjoy one another's company without uttering a word. They were so close that dialogue didn't seem necessary. People that knew them claimed they were the first twin brothers to be born two years apart.

Kevin heard a car enter the garage, a quick tap on the horn. It was Ryan. He waited for the coffee to brew before going down. There were footsteps coming up, smaller steps than Ryan's and Kevin remembered that Ryan had mentioned Allison's school trip. He turned away from the coffee just in time to see his niece enter the office. Her big smile like the morning sun.

"Hey kiddo, how the heck are you doing?" Kevin asked, lifting her off her feet, hugging her tight. He kissed her on the top of her head and then on both cheeks.

Allison giggled as her uncle put her down, gleaming like a brand new toy.

"Where are you going today?" Kevin asked her, as he picked up the coffeepot and led her towards the stairs.

"It's a special trip to the Cloisters," she said, following Kevin downstairs.

"The Cloisters? Do you know that I have never been there?" Kevin said.

"Why not Uncle Kevin?"

"Because I'm your typical New Yorker. I have never been to the Statue of Liberty or the observation deck in the Empire State Building."

"So why does that make you a typical New Yorker?"

"Because we take our landmarks for granted."

"Maybe we should make a trip one day and go all over the city," Allison said, liking her idea very much the second it came out of her mouth.

"Hey that's a great idea," Kevin said, placing the pot of coffee on a small table that stood across from the garage entrance. From there they were able to see who came in and out. It was their dining table and where they had a few beers at the end of the day. "We could pretend we are tourists," he added.

Allison chuckled: "How can we pretend we are tourists if we speak English?"

"Some tourists speak English, but we could get a phony accent," Kevin said, pouring coffee into two mugs lined up like soldiers ready for action. "We could try to speak like Uncle Billy. You know with his heavy Irish brogue. We could tell anyone that asks us that we just came from Ireland for a visit."

Ryan appeared now with a bag from Dunkin Donuts and a cup of juice for Allison.

"What are you guys giggling about?" he asked, sitting on a chair and sipping his coffee.

"We are going as tourists from Ireland all over the city," Kevin said to his brother.

"How hard it is to sound like an Irishman straight from Ireland. You know just like Uncle Billy."

"Me Jaysis you are such an eejit sometime," Ryan said in his perfect Uncle Billy's brogue.

They all broke out laughing, laughter that kept refueling anytime someone said 'Jaysis yeh such a bloody eejit'.

"Well," Ryan said, pushing his mug away after their laughter had faded. He crumbled his napkin and shoved it inside the Dunkin Donuts bag, took a quick glance at his watch. "Ready Allison? We have to go before they leave without you."

Allison wiped her mouth and pushed herself away from the table. She wrapped her arms around Kevin's neck and gave him a kiss on his cheek. "Okay Uncle Kevin," she said, hugging him tight. "Don't forget we are going to be tourists very soon."

"You betcha, honey," he said, putting his arms on her shoulder and walking her to Ryan's truck.

"Now have fun on your trip." He kissed her as he closed the door of the truck and stepped away as Ryan put the truck in drive and drove away.

When Ryan came back, Kevin was already hammering out a few dents on a Honda Prelude. It was eight o' clock.

SEVEN

Papo had placed Lil' Tony in his crib half an hour ago so he could shower. He exited the bathroom and stepped into the room quietly. He paused in front of the crib and stared lovingly at his son. The baby slept peacefully, his tiny chest rising slightly with every breath he took. From behind him Millie's snores reminded him as to why he had to do the job. He walked to the chest of drawers and pulled out a t-shirt and boxers.

He removed the wet towel from around his waist and slipped them on, unhooking the jeans from the back of a chair next to the bed and putting them on. He pulled a hooded sweatshirt over his head, baggy enough to conceal the weapon, and went to the living room and after pulling on a pair of crew socks. Then his boots.

He walked back to the bedroom and retrieved the gun he kept on the top shelf of the closet. He tucked the weapon inside the waistline of his pants and looked at himself in the mirror to check for any noticeable bulging. Satisfied, he smiled and went to his son. He wanted to pick him up and spend the entire day holding him.

He knew that what he was about to do was wrong, but it had to be done. Just one score and it would be enough to skip town, leave New York City altogether. A good friend he had met in prison had offered to help him if he went down to Miami. There was a job waiting for him, a real legit job, and the promise of a place to stay until he found his own.

Damn, even his friend's mother was willing to stay with Lil' Tony while he went out to work. Life was turning out pretty good. But before going legit he had to do one more job, just one more lousy job to give him enough money for the plane fare and a few bucks to keep him and his son fed until his first paycheck.

Papo lowered his head and kissed Lil' Tony's head. It felt cool and the urge to forget about the whole damn deal ran forcefully through his mind again. He didn't have to do anything, but just stay home, where he belonged with his son. Robert would get the idea that he wouldn't be showing up after a good long wait. Robert was stupid, but not stupid enough to wait all day. He didn't give a shit about Robert, anyway.

That was not his concern. His only concern in life was the baby that slept soundly below him. He could always try to borrow enough for the plane fare. He could even call his friend down in Miami and see if he could lend him the money. He would pay it back, they'd both be working together, so it wasn't like he was going to disappear. He could easily hand over most of his pay to his friend until every penny was paid back and didn't have to go out there with a gun strapped to his waist to seek easy cash, someone else's hard earned money.

Papo returned to the living room and paced through the cluttered room, planted himself in front of the window. He pushed the curtain away and stared outside. It was too early for any action on the sidewalks of his neighborhood. Everyone was doing the same thing as Millie, snoring their sorry lives away. To them today was just another day, another lousy day to remind them what losers they were.

People like him and Millie were a bunch of assholes, and a calendar was something they hung up somewhere to add color to their dull lives; free calendars from Chinese takeout restaurants or some cheesy pharmacy where they received their Medicaid pills. He was sick and tired of this life that went nowhere, but to prisons and an early grave.

Yes, he was a product of the streets, a product of lousy schools and a corrupted bureaucracy that did not care about people like him. He was a product of the cold hard streets of New York City, but goddamn didn't he also have a say about the outcome of his life. He did not have to always stay buried under the 'hood.

It was too easy to point fingers at everyone around him and slap them with the responsibility of his life. Yes, that was the easy way of doing things: pass the buck and wipe your hands clean. But didn't he once hear someone preach that when you point a finger at someone, there are always three fingers pointing right back at you?

He stepped away from the window and touched the handle of the gun. Was this the way out of the filthy gutters? Suppose he got arrested and sent back to jail — or even worse — got blown away by another illegal gun kept hidden in someone else's waistband? Was that the type of legacy he was leaving Lil' Tony? — a continuous loser, floating in a never ending cycle of vicious acts.

Papo removed the gun from his waistline and stared at the hardware with close precision. He shuffled to the bedroom and peeked at Lil' Tony. His sweet lips glistened with the drool that fell slowly on his Sesame Street pillow. He closed his eyes and shook his head and took a quick look at the sleeping form of Millie. There was no love for the woman that gave birth to his son and he wondered if there had ever been love there in the first place.

This was not for him, this type of life, and he refused to have his son contaminated by the poison that had contaminated him. "I'm doing this for you, son. The chance I'm taking is worth it. By tomorrow we'll be on a plane on its way to a land of palm trees and blue water beaches."

Papo slipped the gun away, its coldness raising goose bumps on his stomach. He kissed his son for the last time and stepped away from the room. He was about to leave, but then he stopped. He removed a picture of Lil' Tony from the mirror and slipped the photograph into his shirt pocket.

He wanted to have his son next to his heart. He opened the front door and left quietly, never taking a single glance back at the place he would never see again. It was eight o' clock.

EIGHT

The morning dragged into noon. Splashed with a radiant yellow sun, the streets of Brooklyn seemed to sparkle like big golden nuggets. The second week of April and the air already tasted like summer. Music blared through open car windows and people began to empty out from hot apartments and onto building stoops and corner bodegas framed with metal-awnings.

Brooklyn, the largest borough of New York City, and if you listened closely the one that spoke the loudest. Sit with an old timer and they would brag, although in Brooklyn it was not bragging but telling cold solid facts. They would swear in your face that no baseball team was greater than their beloved Brooklyn Dodgers were. Da Bums could have licked the hated

Yankees if it wasn't for the fact that even back then the Yankees bought made-to-order players ala Babe Ruth, rather than grow them the old-fashioned way, through the farm system.

You want to talk about bridges? Man, the bridges of the world begin and end with the Brooklyn Bridge. You're into antiques? Well buddy, if you don't see it on Atlantic Avenue, well it's not an antique yet. And let's not get them started about Nathan's hotdogs or the most famous amusement park in the whole world, Coney Island.

Brooklyn, the home of millions of immigrants that planted roots in its friendly soils, would never become second to none. Not even that piece of pricey concrete filled with uppity-uppity attitudes called Manhattan.

Kevin and Ryan were Brooklynites raised and fed from a close-knit family, a third-generation Irish clan. They grew up like typical kids of their era, filling their time playing Little League baseball sponsored by neighborhood merchants, shooting hoops on the asphalt playground, and mingling with every culture that made the collaged melting pot of Brooklyn so alive and colorful. They were not ones to shun anyone who wasn't Irish. Blacks, Puerto Ricans, West Indians, Jewish, Italian; every other race that stumbled into their backyards formed the neighborhoods.

For that reason the almost daily visit from one of the old timers in the neighborhood delighted them and amused them just the same. His name was Mr. Caruso, an older gentleman with a peculiar disposition and a mouth full of racist tirades that became more like tired jokes, cartoon character dialogue, rather than something to be taken seriously.

The type of man that still called women "broads" and pronounced "oil" with a thick Brooklyn accent that sounded like "earl." An authentic Archie Bunker in living flesh. They always knew whenever Mr. Caruso was in the vicinity because his cigar stench always beat him to the garage. "Hey boys," he would gruff, with a voice that has seen ten thousand cigarettes.

"How you doing, Mr. Caruso?" Kevin asked, always the one to greet him, since he was always closest to the entrance whenever he strolled in—for some reason.

"Fine boys, fine. How's my gal doing? Did you gave her an 'earl' job or you still playing patty cakes with her?"

"Hey, Mr. C," Ryan said, coming around from a transmission job he was almost finished with, on a silver Lexus. "Don't you think this gal should be staying home collecting her pension?"

"That's what's wrong with young guys like you," Mr. Caruso said, moving the cigar from one corner of his mouth to the other, spitting a perfect stream of brown juice from the side of his mouth. "You don't appreciate the workmanship of the old days when cars were built in the good old USA. When cars were rolled out from the plants out in Detroit you knew you weren't buying a car, you were making a lifetime investment. This gal has only 162,000 miles and is still running like the first day I bought her."

Ryan glanced quickly at Kevin, smirked and rolled his eyes. Kevin shrugged his shoulders and shook his head. "Give us till Friday and we'll have your gal ready for another 162,000 miles," Kevin said, snapping his fingers to emphasize the promise that had been made in jest.

"Great, just in time for the weekend. I joined a line-dancing class on Staten Island," Mr. Caruso said, pretending he was holding a dancing partner and gave her a dip.

"Soon I'll be doing Mambo steps better than the Spics."

Ryan closed his eyes and mumbled a Jesus under his breath, always dreading the racist names that spurted from the old man's mouth.

"You boys ate lunch already?" Mr. Caruso asked, relighting his cigar, which had somehow gone out.

"You want me to run over to the diner and pick you up some decent lunch or are you Micks still dunking soda bread in Jack Daniels for your liquid lunches?"

"No thanks, Mr. C," Ryan replied, ignoring the racial slur that came out of Mr. Caruso's mouth with the same tone someone would say "bless you" upon hearing you sneeze. "We just finished having some pizza, but thanks anyway."

Mr. Caruso walked around inspecting the work that both brothers were doing, taking a peek inside the open hood the Lexus. He returned to his original spot and spit out another streak of tobacco juice.

"I saw your mother the other day at the A&P. You boys have a looker for a mom and her gams," he said, positioning his hands in front of his chest as if squeezing a woman's breasts. "They are still nice enough to give an old man like me lasting dreams. Too bad you boys don't favor her good looks—you both got nasty mugs, as if a gorilla fathered you."

The brothers once again glanced at each other with quizzical looks as if to say "does this man stop at nothing with the insults?"

Wasn't anything sacred for Mr. Caruso? But they paid him no mind, since for all the foul remarks that came out of him, he meant no harm. He was as harmless as an old dog with no teeth, no bark and a limp for a walk. He was an old man with nothing better to do with his retired self, but walk around the neighborhood visiting local merchants that tolerated his antics.

Even when his car did not need service, he stopped by almost every day to shoot the breeze and to remind them that there were still people that favored the brutish old-school racist way of thinking.

"Okay, boys," Mr. Caruso said, raising his hand to wave goodbye. "I'll see ya Friday. Remember to give your best to my gal. Make her shiny and new."

"Take care Mr. C," Ryan said, nodding.

"Stay out of trouble, Mr. Caruso," Kevin said, patting the old man on his shoulder as he left.

Mr. Caruso, with his dyed jet-black-coiffed hair, emulating his idol Steve McGarrett from the old 70s show "Hawaii 5-0", waved again and exited, his cigar smoked lingering in the garage like a nuclear cloud.

"Me Jaysis, wha' a bloody eejit," Ryan said, sounding like his Uncle Billy and getting back to work.

"Poor bastard,"" Kevin laughed. "I guess neither one of us wanted to tell him his fly was open."

"Shit," Ryan said, smirking. "Don't be surprised if he did it on purpose just to be a nuisance to any woman that passes by."

"Jaysis, you're right. A bloody eejit he is," Kevin said, continuing in his Uncle Billy's voice.

They both laughed, laughing harder when they shot a glare at Mr. Caruso's old gal, a dull maroon Plymouth that sat like some forgotten dinosaur in the Museum of Natural History.

NINE

Papo slid next to Robert in a booth at McDonalds. Robert was already stuffing a handful of fries into his mouth, which was already packed with half-chewed cheeseburger. It was disgusting seeing him shove his food into his mouth like a sanitation truck; it could ruin anyone's appetite. The fast food restaurant was at its peak with kids running zigzag everywhere and mothers trying to corral them like cattle. Young lovers shared a burger and a milkshake and to Papo it reminded him of when he and Millie had something going on, before she became pregnant and everything twisted into an affair spawned in hell.

He looked the other way to avoid looking at Robert as he watched the people walk by from the other side of the large glass window. He envied them as they strolled by with easy steps that told everyone they had a decent comfortable life. Before long he would be walking like that too, with a leisurely step and let some other loser envy him from the inside of another fast food joint.

"Come on bro, fuck you gonna do? Spend the whole fuckin' day stuffin' your mouth?" Papo asked, anxious to get this shit over with.

"Slow down, G. I'll be done soon, so chill man," Robert said, with his mouth full, making his words sound foreign.

"Coño bro, swallow that shit before talkin'. You're almost making me puke."

Robert raised his hand and motioned to wait as he swallowed hard and gulped the soda, pushing all the solid food down. "Yo, Papo, what's the hurry? Didn't you say that the best time was to hit them at the end of the day? Damn man, is not even one, chill out and have a burger."

Papo stared at Robert hard, wondering if having this fool as his helper was the best idea he could come up with. Robert lacked common sense and his nasty drug habit made him unreliable. But he was the best in this situation and knew how to keep his mouth shut.

Papo knew that he was also afraid of him and he used that to his advantage. But nevertheless he was itching to start and finish this last job as quickly as possible.

"Listen," Papo said in a low voice.

There were too many people around and it angered him that he allowed Robert to choose the meeting place before the job. "Let's get the fuck outta here. Too many nosy ears, know what I mean?"

Robert looked around, as if realizing for the first time that almost every table had been taken by someone stuffing in calories and calories of greasy junk. He stood up and left the mess he'd created on the plastic red tray, walked out.

"Yo bro," Papo called out. "What the fuck you think you got fuckin' maids here? Empty this shit where it belongs. Nobody wants to touch your shit that fell out your mouth."

Robert stopped and looked at the table, embarrassed that Papo had come out with such loud humiliating remarks. He wanted to tell him that people got the minimum wage here just to do that, pick up after slobs like him, but he didn't like the look that Papo had in his eyes ever since he'd arrived.

He buttoned his mouth and like a well-trained dog straight out of obedience school picked up his tray and dumped the ketchup-laced place mat and greasy bags in the garbage can that stood by the exit door.

Outside the weather was heating up and it seemed like the entire borough of Brooklyn was jam-packed on the sidewalks around them. A car roared by that played the theme song of "The Godfather" when the driver blew the horn.

"Yo man, listen up," Papo said, chastising Robert as they bopped down Pacific Street, heading out to Atlantic Avenue. "We gotta be cool what we said out in public. After today there's gonna be a lot of heat coming down. The fewer people hear what we about to do, the less chances the cops will trace our asses. We can't go on and score with this job and then go out and start telling every motherfucker out there that we did it. Know what I mean? After we do our shit we have to stay low, low bro like a fuckin' snake. The second we say any shit, the cops are gonna be down our fuckin' throats. So you got to be cool. Know what I'm sayin'?"

Robert nodded as he walked with his eyes paying keen attention to how his feet shuffled in the smooth rhythm of his paces. He guessed Papo was right, the last thing he wanted was to get caught, this was no little break-in and stealing someone's toaster — this was the equivalent of breaking into the White House and stealing the President's coffee mug.

They walked in silence through the streets of Brooklyn, passing drivers with little patience to wait for pedestrians to cross the streets. They turned on Dean Street and went from Fourth Avenue towards Third Avenue. At the corner of Dean and Third they stopped and looked to their left, as a car pulled out of the garage.

They watched an old man walk in as a boy zipped by on a fast red ten-speed bike. It was the perfect spot to check out the garage. From this position they could see the movements inside the shadowy garage and made sure the two mechanics were in there by themselves.

Papo looked around and unlike Fourth Avenue and Pacific Street and the whole area of Atlantic Avenue that was packed with shoppers and loiterers, things were quiet, even isolated, on Third Avenue. All was going as planned, though he had hoped for a drizzly, cloudy day unlike today. There was something about a summer-like day in the beginning of April that made every bastard want to be out in the street.

Papo wondered if he should have planned to hit the garage early in the morning rather than late afternoon. Well, it was too late and he'd already gotten the information about the tickets to Miami. There was a flight leaving that night and another departing early in the morning. He figured the best flight was tomorrow's, which would give him time to buy the ticket and go home and pack a bag for Lil' Tony. Just the essentials as he was planning to travel light. There was going to be enough money there to buy new clothes for both of them when they got to Miami.

Like Millie wouldn't suspect what he was up to until he was already on the plane heading to real palm trees, something he had never seen before. The thought of white, clean, sandy beaches and warm winds stroking tall palms made him relax and smile. Papo thought of skipping town without splitting the loot with Robert, but he knew that Robert could go to the cops and rat him out. He watched Robert closely, the man was beginning to shake and there was a sickly pale color to his face. He had the look of a man ready to faint or shit in his pants.

Robert was petrified and that was the last thing Papo needed, a terrified person always made stupid mistakes. Something he couldn't afford, not when Miami was just around the corner.

A cop car was cruising by and Papo was able to see it when it was just one block away. He straightened up and motioned Robert to start walking.

"Come on. Let's move. The cops are comin' and if they see us standin' here doin' shit they might stick around a little longer. Or worse come around more times than they were plannin' to."

They walked past the entrance of the garage and heard laughter and muffled conversation. The old man that they had seen before was still there and Papo couldn't help noticing the guy's hair. It was the type of hairdo that took a few hours to sculpt and a lot of hair spray or God-knows-what to keep it stiff.

Shit, Papo thought, if any bugs were flying around they were sure to tack on to the old geezer's sticky coiffure. He chuckled, for it reminded him of his Aunt Tita every time she came back from the beauty parlor. It was like a religious thing for her, every Saturday morning without fail, rain or shine, for all seasons. She would get up and march to the beauty parlor across the street from the apartment she shared with his mother and all the kids from both sisters.

The beauty parlor was a tiny hole in the wall owned by a Dominican woman who always looked like a mannequin ready to be displayed in a Macy's window. Every man from the neighborhood used to parade by just to get a glimpse of her huge butt. Man, even the kids approaching puberty used to ogle her and then probably run home to the bathroom to pull on their little wieners. She was that fine, well not exactly fine, she just oozed the type of lust that made you want to be hurt by her.

So every Saturday morning his aunt would go to the Dominican hairdresser, and after several hours would come back to the house with a high hairdo that resembled a dome, stiff like a bronzed beehive. The kids took turns throwing little rolled up balls of paper to see whose would ricochet the farthest. Any ball that remained trapped in the hair got extra points.

While all this was happening, Aunt Tita remained clueless and had no idea her head had become a target, like an Olympic marathon going on all weekend. Papo felt like laughing, wondering what her reaction would be after finding little paper balls stuck to her hair late Thursday, when the hairdo began to break down.

They walked around the block and Papo was getting antsy, it was now or never. They came around Dean Street again and went to Third Avenue, keeping surveillance of the garage from across the street rather than the corner where they couldn't see much of the action that was going on. The old man was leaving and

Papo's heart almost went into cardiac arrest, the time had come.

No more ifs or buts, the time he'd been thinking of for the past week has arrived and there was nothing in hell that would make him chicken out. He glimpsed at Robert and saw the sweat coming from underneath the man's scalp. Yep, the asshole was scared and Papo hoped that this was not some omen, for him to squash the whole plan. Maybe get a better partner in crime than this bastard that seemed to be shaking like a fucking leaf on a windy autumn night.

Well, there was no time for that, the ballgame was about to begin regardless if one had the best players on the field or not. As the umpire in his mind shouted, "Let's play BALL!!"

TEN

Robert was nervous. He could feel the tumbling in his stomach as a streak of sweat traced the line of his spine. He puffed on his cigarette and looked the other way, away from Papo, and across the street where he could see the dimmed doorway that framed the front of the car repair shop. He inhaled a deep drag from the Marlboro and held the smoke in his mouth. He could taste the nicotine and could feel the smoke as it began to tickle the inside of his nose.

He exhaled slowly, hoping to calm his nerves. He wanted so bad to take a shit. He glanced at Papo to see if his buddy was nervous, his friend was not showing it. Then again it was Papo's idea and leaving jail just two weeks before, Papo was not afraid of another visit behind bars.

But not he, not the middle son of Mrs. Garcia that was once the darling of the family, but now the disgrace of the entire Garcia clan. He could swear on a stack of Bibles that he was petrified about the thought of jail. He was scared, no, more than scared, he was terrified. So why the hell didn't he just turn around and leave Papo to do his little scheme by himself? It shouldn't have been so hard, damn it. Just turn around and go the hell back home. Robert shifted his weight, fidgeting like a little kid. He leaned to his right, like a base runner getting ready to steal second base.

Papo turned around and stared at him. In his eyes Robert saw danger and a devil-to-hell- attitude. Robert saw the consequences of deciding to just squash their plans in Papo's intense black eyes. Or as they said when they were kids, if he left him flat.

"Give me a cigarette," Papo said. Something Robert always hated about his so-called friend. It was as if the word please or the simple task of asking pleasantly was alien to Papo's vocabulary and mannerisms. But like the punk and the follower he was, Robert obeyed as he dug into his pack and gave

Papo a cigarette. Papo locked the stick between his lips and leaned forward, an indication that not only was Robert supposed to supply the cigarette, but he must supply the light as well.

"Yo bro," Papo said, taking a long drag from the cigarette. "What's up with you? You look like shit."

Robert forced a laugh, which sounded like a girlish giggle. "I'm cool, bro. Don't worry about me. I just want to get this shit over with, you know what I mean?"

Papo sized him up from behind a cloud of smoke, his right eyebrow raised upward in a perfect arch. It was something Papo started doing after watching Mr. Spock on old reruns of Star Trek. He didn't realize that it made him look stupid, like a lost, scared boy pretending to be tough.

"Just watch my back, bro, and don't get stupid on me. You know what I'm saying? Whatever you do, don't fuck up. This is going to be sweet and easy. A bang-bang thank you ma'am kind of a shit. Those white boys ain't going to do nothin' but just drop their pants and give us the bills. We'll be in and out in less than five minutes."

"What about if they don't have any money?" Robert asked, hoping his question would make Papo abort the robbery.

Papo glared at Robert and flung the cigarette butt with disgust into the garbage littered gutter. "What's up with you, bro? Those boys got money. Shit man, they have cars coming in and out like fuckin' roaches in the night. There must be a few grand inside that garage. A few grand that would look better in our pockets rather than theirs so stop thinking like that. Even better, don't fuckin' think, just stay there and let me do the job."

Robert looked away and leaned against a parked car, hoping the alarm was the sensitive type. That would start screeching the second someone tapped the hood. He figured that if the car alarm went off, it might make Papo forget about the robbery plan. But the car remained silent as a smashed car in a junk yard.

Annoyed, he stepped away from it as he closed his eyes and lifted his face up into the sun. The rays felt warm and soothing and all he wanted was to let the sun massage him and allow him to forget about Papo's chilling look. Why he even listened to Papo was beyond him. And for that he chastised himself for his weakness, a weakness which was surely going to someday place him in a very nasty situation.

Robert had just bumped into Papo only two nights before and though he'd been tired and heading home, he allowed Papo to talk him into a few beers in front of the schoolyard by his house. Papo was not the type of person you considered a friend, but an acquaintance. Just a nobody from the neighborhood that was bad news. Not that Robert was a saint, but next to Papo, he was one fitting away from getting a golden halo and white satin robe.

Papo had a nasty streak ever since they both met in Mrs. Foster's second grade classroom. By the time Papo was twelve he had seen the insides of juvenile delinquent headquarters enough times to know where every bathroom was. When he reached the age of twenty he graduated to a small cell overlooking the waters that surround Riker's Island.

On the other hand, Robert considered himself a nice passive guy that was only into petty crimes that hurt nobody. A break-in in someone's house to steal small items, which he got rid of quickly, didn't hurt anyone. It was not like he was a killer or a rapist, was the way he justified his actions. He was a two-bit criminal caught only twice for possession of small quantities of drugs.

And thanks to the leniency of the justice system, he received a summons and a slap on the wrist both times. But it had also made him cautious, even though his crack habit fueled his criminal behavior. He always made sure to stay one step ahead of the law.

"Ready?" Papo asked, clearing his throat hard and spitting on the ground.

He crossed the street and Robert followed.

"Okay bro, let me do the talkin'. All I want you to do is stay close. Just make sure they see the knife and look at them hard. Remember, if we get them by surprise those motherfuckers ain't gonna to do shit, but cough up the money. They ain't stupid, the last thing they want is a bullet up their ass."

Both men moved closer to the garage, the early afternoon sun falling lazily on the street. Specks of glass embedded in the pavement sparkled like tiny fallen stars. Robert felt his steps echo like a distant afterthought in his head. Everything moved ever so slowly, in a surrealistic train of thought. It felt like a dream taking final shape, or even better, an out-of-body experience.

He felt cold, clammy perspiration dotting his forehead and his throat became tight, making it impossible to breath. They entered the garage; the shadows inside blinding them with darkness. It was like walking into a movie house after a movie had started, until their pupils focused and restored their vision. Two cars were lifted high above the oil-stained floor and another was parked to the side, its hood open wide like a giant mouth frozen during a stiff yawn.

"Can I help you guys?" someone asked, the voice coming from across the doorway.

Robert and Papo stepped into the middle of the shop. Robert could feel his heart pumping as if it went into overdrive in the weight room at the gym. His breath was stale and tasted like dirty pennies. He stared at the young mechanic that stood in front of them wiping his fingers with a soiled rag.

"How you doing guys?" he said to them, a thin friendly smile spreading across his lips. Robert bit his lower lip wondering why Papo was not doing what he had said he was going to do, to do the talking. The plan began to unravel. He realized that Papo, regardless of his tough talk and bullshit, was as scared as he was, maybe even more.

"Where's your car? It's really that bad that it didn't even make it this far, eh?" the young mechanic asked, joking and slipping the rag in his back pocket.

"Say something, bro," Robert said to Papo in Spanish, afraid that if he spoke in English the mechanic would know what they were trying to do.

"Carajo, don't go faggot on me now," Papo responded in Spanish, his eyes never leaving the young mechanic.

"Hey fellas," the mechanic said, lifting one hand in. "I'm a bit busy, so can I help you with something? Otherwise I'll have to ask you to leave."

"Like fuck we are," Papo said, whipping the gun out. The barrel a few inches from the startled mechanic's face. "Now be cool motherfucker or I'll blow your ass up right now."

"Okay, okay man," the young man said, raising his hands. "I'm cool. Just go easy with that gun. Whatever you want, buddy you got it, just be cool with that gun."

"Where's the fuckin' money?" Papo asked, waving the gun.

The mechanic began to lower his hand toward his pocket.

"Keep your fuckin' hands up!" Papo said, saliva spraying out of his twisted mouth.

"I'm cool, man. I'm just trying to give you my wallet," the mechanic said, reasoning.

"I'm giving you the money. That's what you want, right?"

"Fuck your bullshit money," Papo said, poking the mechanic's chest with the gun. "We want the real money. You think we're stupid? Now where the fuck is the real money?"

The mechanic moistened his lips as Papo came closer. "Where's your partner? I know he's still here and no funny stuff 'cause I'll plug your ass right here and now."

A creak of footsteps from above them was heard before he could answer. Papo looked up and grinned. "Okay, bro. Let's go upstairs and see if your buddy knows where the real money is at."

All three climbed the stairs and when they reached the landing the other mechanic poked his head through the small doorway of the tiny office. He asked a question, but became silent the second he saw the gun and the two intruders barging in. Papo pushed the first mechanic toward the other one and then pointed the gun with stern authority. He saw the safe and his lips curved into a satisfied smile.

"Okay, open that fuckin' safe and no stupid superhero shit. Just give us the money and everything will be cool. Robert," Papo barked at his partner without turning. "Any one of these motherfuckers move, slice them up like fuckin' cold cuts. Now come on asshole," he said as the mechanic got closer to the

179

safe. "Open that safe and give us all you got and I fuckin' know there's a lot."

Robert stared at the two mechanics wondering if he had the guts to use the knife if it came to that. Everything was moving fast, as if someone had hit a button in his head and the speed was in super-fast forward. He felt the sweat all over his body shooting out of his pores in freezing streams. Papo was in front of him and from the top of his buddy's shoulders Robert could see one of the mechanics, the one that was in the office when they came in. He turned and kneeled in front of the safe.

Robert heard the clicks and spins of the combination lock. The speed button in his mind switched to super slow. Even Papo's voice, his cursing commands was just a distant muffle that fell on his ears. Then something happened and the speed in his mind was once again changed, distorted as the mechanic that had knelt in front of the safe opened the door and removed the money. He also took a canvas bag from the safe and stuffed the cash inside.

He handed it to Papo and Robert.

Thank God. All they had to do now was get the hell out of there. Robert took a few steps towards the door expecting that Papo would do the same. Come on, back away slowly and in no time they would be outside running to salvation. But wait, what the hell was wrong with Papo?

Robert stopped and glared at Papo's back. He waved the money bag in the air and pointed the gun from one mechanic to the other. "I want it all motherfuckers," Papo screamed, saliva shooting out in a twisted, disgusting rainbow.

"That's all we have," the mechanic said, his voice strong, without a trace of fear.

Papo scowled from one mechanic to the other and spat on the floor. He shook his head in disbelief. "You think I'm some stupid fuckin' spic? Fuck you, you white motherfuckers! Now you better give me more money or this asshole is going down first," Papo yelled, swinging the gun at the head of the mechanic standing on the other side.

"Okay, okay. Easy man, easy," the mechanic said, lifting his hands while glancing at the other mechanic with a look of protection.

"Okay dude, easy with that gun. I'll give you everything we have." He turned around and knelt in front of the safe, his arms reaching inside, all the way in deep.

Papo turned to Robert and grinned, like a sneaky cat that just swallowed a canary and a goldfish. He gave the bag to Robert and winked.

Robert took the money and clutched it tight to his chest, the small bundle next to his palpitating heart. He relaxed. This was easy, Robert heard his mind whisper to him. If it's really this easy a few more of these jobs could put some serious bills in his pocket. He felt himself relax as he glanced at the two mechanics, feeling compassion for them.

Suddenly it occurred to him that they looked alike and the thought crossed his mind that perhaps they were brothers. He felt a touch of sadness, but squeezed the bag closer to him. That emotion changed into a giddiness of greed and selfishness. Robert allowed himself to smile and the anticipation of splitting the money and the partying they were going to do was worth everything he had gone through.

Then a flash popped in front of his eyes, almost like an unexpected flash from a camera. His mind exploded into disjointed movements. Once again the speed button went into super-fast forward. He was clueless of what was going on and his mind replayed in nanoseconds what had occurred. The mechanic rummaging inside the safe had a gun.

There was a ringing in Robert's ears, as if someone had blown off a firecracker inside his head. Robert saw Papo fall. Not just falling but propelled off his feet. His partner was down, down on the floor in a sickening, slow fatal dance. Blood sprayed from Papo's face, thick red liquid spurting out in quick sprinkles, and it didn't look like the tomato ketchup in Clint Eastwood cowboy movies.

This was real, and somehow the easy job, the stealing of a lollipop from a baby turned into a war of survival. Robert heard Papo fall, a loud thump that seemed to shake the entire building. Robert ran to his left and spun quickly, realizing he was running toward the wall. He was disoriented, confused, could not focus, and his heartbeat was a loud, hammering pain that wanted to burst out of his chest. He ran to his right and then like a spinning toy cranked to its maximum potential, he ran in short circles, terrified that a bullet would find his ass and make him join Papo to a trip straight to hell.

He saw the door and bolted toward it, his feet feeling submerged in molasses. He bit down on his lower lip to stop it from trembling, but realized that his entire body shook. Not just his lip. He ran down the stairs almost losing balance. He missed the last step and twisted his ankle. He felt the pain, but ignored it as he dashed like a lunatic track runner in a furious attempt to get to the finish line.

He ran into the bright sunshine expecting any second the biting sting of a bullet would crash into him. He ran, he ran like mad and when he was out of breath, he stopped and discovered he was almost ten to twelve blocks away. He let out a long breath of relief and before he knew it, he collapsed on a building stoop. He dropped his face into his hands and thanked God, but somehow he knew that God didn't want any part of his tainted praise.

For the first time since he'd run out of the garage, Robert noticed the canvas bag of money. He peeked inside and looked solemnly at the bills. How much sweat and hard labor had it taken to make this fortune? Robert didn't know and he didn't want to contemplate it. He thought about Papo and knew he was dead. Blown away. Shot in the head at close range. It had been a gruesome picture of death. In his mind he kept seeing Papo flying in the air and crashing to the ground. *Goddamn asshole*, Robert wanted to scream. This was enough, you goddam greedy bastard.

Robert stood but the pain forced him to sit down again. He wanted to get the hell out of there, anywhere as far away as possible. He could still smell the gunpowder mixed with the stink of flesh and singed hair. He could still see the blood splashing about like a macabre fountain. He wanted to forget the whole day. If he could only press some magic button and erase everything that had happened those last few hours.

Even if it meant not having the money that he now rocked close to his chest.

He stood up and his ankle screamed out in pain and he almost stumbled on the pavement. He started to walk, gingerly, for now the adrenaline rush he had felt throughout his body was no longer there. He wanted to get high and let the powers of crack launch him out of reality and into the stratosphere. And that was what Robert did. He found his way to a nonstop binge that kept him flying higher and higher into numbness and depleted the hard earned money of two mechanics into almost nothing.

By the time the cops tracked him down, Robert's mind was a useless piece of fried brain tissue. And inside the bowels of a Riker's jail cell, he sat wondering over and over where the hell he went wrong. At least, he nodded to himself, the innocent were not hurt. And with that thought he went to sleep, oblivious to the fact that the lives of two hardworking men were forever destroyed by the stupid actions of two imbeciles looking for a quick payday minus the sweat of an honest day's work.

ELEVEN

Kevin stared at the crumpled body that lay at his feet. There was a big reddish burnt hole where a face was supposed to be. He was still holding the gun and it felt hot, as if he was holding a coal just removed from a barbecue pit. In the distance he heard the muffled sounds of sirens and the softness in his brother's voice. He wanted to look away, away from the body, the body of a man that just a few minutes ago was a live human being. He killed a man, the realization came to him slowly. Is this man heading towards heaven or hell? Kevin closed his eyes, but he could still see the body. It would stay there forever, a graphic Polaroid, an inescapable image.

He allowed Ryan to take him and lead him away from the small tiny hole that they so proudly called the office, since they decided on opening their own repair shop. Brother and brother like always, doing everything together. No army could beat them as long as they stood together, back-to-back ready to battle hell itself. And that was what happened. They had met their opposition and like united blood brothers were victorious, like when they challenged anybody for a game of hoop or a round of stickball at the schoolyard.

My God, I just took the life of a man, Kevin kept repeating over and over like a dull headache that refused to go away. This was not a stickball game they had been playing, this was no basketball game played at St. Mary's gym, this was real life and death, a deadly game with no rules but whoever was still standing won. Simple as that, no consolation prize given to the loser. Just six cold dirty feet of isolation. Forever and ever.

Kevin looked around and saw the cars still waiting for their skills and attention scattered around them like a silent audience waiting to applaud or laugh or cry. How the hell had he gotten down there? He asked himself and without waiting for his brain to give him the answer he disposed of such frivolous bullshit and concentrated more on the man that had just become a spirit in the safe confines of their humble little greasy garage.

"Give me the gun," Ryan had said softly. "Give me the gun and keep your mouth shut."

Kevin stared at Ryan and for the first time, he cared for him. He felt proud of his little brother and wanted to put his arms around him and kiss him and tell him that he loved him. And at that moment he realized he had never shown any emotion like that and wondered if he should do it or if it was uncalled for especially among real bad-ass Irish men.

He had never told Ryan about the gun. He knew how Ryan had felt about firearms, shit even as kids, Ryan was never into playing cowboys and Indians. He had bought the gun from Frankie, a local guy that always seemed to be at the bar, in his usual spot, shooting the breeze and never swallowing more than two light beers a night. Frankie was the type of guy you always wanted to keep as a friend and never, God forbid, never cross the man and make him your enemy.

Had it been a mistake buying the gun? For killing a man without at least trying to disarm him? If he didn't have the gun, would the robber have left with the bit of money that was inside the safe? How much was there anyway? A few hundred dollars? Maybe a thousand? Goddamnit, didn't those assholes know that it was the era of plastic money and promised checks from car insurance companies that would be mailed within the next three business days? Who the hell kept cash on their premises anymore? Nobody unless you were a check cashing place. Why them, goddamnit? Why them? Goddamn stupid assholes! Me Jaysis, wha' bloody fuckin' eejits.

Kevin felt Ryan shaking him from side to side. "Come on Kevin, snap out of it. Fuck…the cops are already here, just listen, just fucking listen. Remember the gun belongs to the other robber that got away with the money. You were able to wrestle the gun from him and shot the other punk. It was self-defense, do you hear me Kevin? It was fucking self-defense. Just let me handle the cops and stick to my story."

"Okay, Ryan," Kevin mumbled, opening his eyes wide as if trying to pull in all the reality that the day had to offer, to rid himself of the nightmare that had just occurred. "I love you, bro'," Kevin mumbled again, but Ryan was no longer by his side as he was walking to meet the two cops that were entering the garage.

"Hey officers," Kevin heard Ryan speak in a respectful voice. "My name is Ryan and this is my brother Kevin. We were robbed by two men, one got away with some money. I don't know exactly how much and the other guy is dead upstairs. They both had guns, my brother was able to take one gun from one of them and in self-defense shot him in the face."

The two cops, their nametags right above their shields. Officer Doyle and Officer Hernandez. They looked up in unison as if expecting to see the body dangling from the ceiling, then glanced at Kevin. "Is he okay?" Officer Hernandez asked as he walked closer to Kevin. "Hey buddy, are you all right?"

Kevin was feeling more like his old self as he nodded trying to put some assurance on the stare he returned to the cop. "As best as possible. I'm still a bit shook up, but yeah, I'm okay...thanks."

"So what happened?" Officer Hernandez asked.

Kevin knew exactly what he was doing. Trying to see the consistency of the story. "Just like my brother said," Kevin said, massaging the back of his neck, feeling tightness beginning to annoy him. "I was upstairs taking care of some paperwork when my brother was pushed inside the office and two guys with guns were demanding our money."

"Why didn't you just give them the money and let them go away?" Officer Doyle asked nonchalantly.

"We did," Kevin said a bit louder. "When I gave him everything we had in the safe he wasn't satisfied, so he began to shout that he wanted more and pointed the gun at my brother, threatening to blow his head off."

Officer Hernandez sized Kevin up, shot a glimpse at Ryan, and returned his attention to Kevin. "Is that when you took the gun from the other one and blew his partner away?"

Kevin nodded trying not to give too many quick answers. "Yes, something like that...you have to understand that everything happened so fast. I'm still in shock that it really happened."

There were more sirens approaching the block as people from the neighborhood began to gather outside the garage, stretching their necks to see who would be the first one to get a grasp of what was going on. Within minutes the place resembled a scene straight out of a cops and robbers television show. The garage was now inundated with cops and both brothers knew that it would not be long before the plainclothes cops arrived.

If they thought that the grilling they were getting from the first two officers was tough, they had no idea what was in store for them from the more seasoned detectives. Both Kevin and Ryan led Officers Doyle and Hernandez upstairs to the office and the second Kevin entered, the whole nightmare jumped at him and grabbed him by the throat. He almost vomited the two pepperoni slices he had for lunch. The stench was maddening and he wondered why he was the only one that seemed to be affected by it. He looked quickly at Ryan and his brother was standing with the cops as if all three men were contemplating over beers if they should flip the smoking, well done steaks in a backyard barbecue.

He could see the dead man's legs. They were twisted…in a way that should have been comical. He was wearing Timberland boots, the laces hanging untied like beige licorice strings. He was younger than him and Ryan, early twenties, and already a statistic on the blotters of the New York Police Department. *Was life that cheap for these people?* Kevin asked himself.

But he couldn't categorize an entire Hispanic race by two morons that decided to go for a quick get-rich scheme. Damn one of his best friends was a Puerto Rican fellow that every Christmas made sure to bring him *pasteles*, a delicious meat pie that was a typical Puerto Rican delicacy for the season. And the yellow rice and roasted pork. Damn his friend's families were all great college-educated people that respected the law as much as his own. Crime was something that did not discriminate, all races and creeds were welcome to its domain.

"Kevin...Yo' Kevin," Ryan came to his brother and squeezed his arm. "Come on let's go down, the cops do not want anyone upstairs until the detectives arrive. They don't wanna disturb the crime scene."

Kevin stared at Ryan, witnessing his strength. He hated Ryan now for the way he was taking charge, leading him around as if he was a pony giving rides to local city kids during a street fair. Doesn't he realized that he just killed a man? Most likely these fucking cops, these two bumbling cops have never fired their fucking guns except in the firing range. How the fuck do any of these motherfuckers know how he feels?

Killing a man in the middle of the afternoon is not something that you could do and then go to the nearest bar and throw down a few cold ones and do the play by play commentary. There goes Kevin he points, he shoots...yesssssss...Kevin scores...good guys one...bad guys nothing. Boy, Skip this is turning into a real old-fashioned duel. Well we'll be right back, but first another word from our sponsors Smith and

Wesson…*when you want the job to be done right the first time reach out for the one with the loud pop.*

They descended and the garage was covered in a sea of blue. It seemed like every cop on duty in Brooklyn was present. They stood in little scattered bunches as if waiting for butlers to bring them hors d'oeuvres at a cocktail party. Four men made their way through the cops and the second they entered, every uniformed man stood a bit more erect, a bit more busy even if it meant looking at the inside of the cars waiting for repair. Kevin followed them with his eyes as they stopped in front of them and suddenly he knew they had taken charge, just like the cavalry arriving to kick some serious butt.

"What we got here?" one of them asked, his trained eyes giving Kevin and Ryan a quick up and down strip stare. Officer Hernandez filled them in and after that both Officers Doyle and Hernandez vanished from the investigation. Just like that, with the swiftness of a snap of the finger. "Come with us please," the same detective said, the please just a formality with no real conviction, like a doctor trying to give his best bedside manners, but coming off as real as a three dollar bill.

"Excuse me officer," Kevin said, noticing that the officer's comment did not go too well with the detective. But to the man's credit he did not correct him. "But if you don't mind I'd rather stay here. I can't stand seeing that dead man again."

The detective nodded, his eyebrows bunching up with an understanding look and all of a sudden he looked human, just like any other person in a room of strangers. Kevin felt at ease with him and he relaxed, feeling his true self finally taking command. "You see sir, I was the one that pulled the trigger, and it was the first time that I ever held a gun in my life. I'm a stranger to this whole shit, if I go up to that office again I know I'm going to get sick."

"Very well," the detective said with a warm smile. Kevin knew that this was a person he could feel comfortable with, hanging out talking about the Yankees' chances of winning the World Series again over a few beers and pretzels.

"I'll come with you guys," Ryan volunteered. "We were both together."

Kevin saw them march up as he leaned on a car realizing that it was Mr. Caruso's old gal and knowing that this old gal was not getting near the Verrazano Bridge to Staten Island anytime soon. *Well*, he thought almost laughing out loud, *Mr. Caruso is going to have to wait to learn those mambo steps.*

Officer Hernandez came to him, his hat in his hands showing off his receding hairline. In the next few years this man was going to be bald. "You look better," he commented. "Hell of a way to end the day, eh?"

Kevin forced a smile, but was not too successful. "Tell me about it, and of all days I was heading home to take my wife out for dinner."

"Really, any special occasion?"

"Just to assure her that I love her very much," Kevin said, shocked that those words came out of his mouth. To him those words sounded hollow, like the corny dialogue of a cheesy soap opera. He felt embarrassed saying them.

Officer Hernandez acknowledged the sentimentality, but let it drop as if he understood Kevin's display of uneasiness. "We just got some information from headquarters, just between us two...okay, I'm not even supposed to tell you this, but I figure it might ease you a bit. That punk upstairs was a loser from the get. He just came out of jail two weeks ago after serving six months for attempted robbery. Just try not to let it get to you... it was either you, your brother or him. You had no choice, but the right one. I know exactly how you feel. It's never too easy to face the fact that your actions were responsible for taking a life. Loser or not, taking a life is only God's job, but sometimes even God does not give you any choices, you just have to react and hope that it's to the best of your judgment. I took a life once, and to this day I think about it, but I know that because of my actions I am still able to kiss my wife and kids hello every day. Here's my card if you ever need anything, even someone to bullshit about it, feel free to call."

The detectives came down; Ryan holding the rear as Officer Hernandez patted Kevin on the arm and then went to join his partner. Kevin slipped the card into his overall's pocket and faced the group of detectives and Ryan that were now standing close to him. "Your brother just gave us his statement. We're going to need a statement from you too, but you could always come down to the precinct tomorrow. Are you okay?" the detective said with concern. "Here's my number. I'm Detective Higgins. You might want to consult your lawyer, not that you did anything wrong, but there will be an investigation and sometimes you get assholes from headquarters trying to find a snowball buried beneath the sands of Coney Island in the middle of summer. It's for your own peace of mind."

"Thank you, Detective Higgins, I appreciate that very much," Kevin said, adding another cop card to his collection. He watched the detectives march outside and now two men from the Coroner's office climbed the stairs with a shiny black body-bag and a stretcher and Kevin wanted to get the hell out of here. Get as far away as possible because the last thing he wanted to see was somebody being dragged down in a morbid body bag.

He couldn't breathe and took his face into his hands and swore that his entire head was going to explode. He would have paid a million dollars to have been able to scream from the top of his lungs. Ryan came to him and for the first time in his life Kevin crumbled in the strong arms of his little brother and he cried.

TWELVE

Tick, tack, tick, tack, the clock moved with no concern for its own time. Just tick, tock, tick, tock...like a monotonous song of a drunken fool that only knew the first four words of the lyrics and that was all. He stared at the darkness hearing the maddening voice of time moving slowly, as an urge to take a hammer to it rushed through him. Forget the hammer. He would have been very comfortable killing the clock with his bare hands. Too bad he didn't have a gun, otherwise he would have blown it away in one instant. The sound effect would have been more than enough for the price of admission.

BANG!

Tick, tock, tick, tock...

Kevin passed his fingers through his hair almost pulling each strand out by its roots. Tick, tock, tick, tock...he closed his fingers into a fist and clenched them with all his might. He could feel his nails digging sharply into the meaty part of his palms. He welcomed the pain, but not the sound of time passing by. At almost five in the morning he would give up the search for sleep and would began to get ready to go to work at seven. How much longer could his body take this? He had no idea, but until he learned the answer he would abuse his body and brain until then.

Every night was the same; insomnia became his companion during those witching hours when the ticking of the clock took control of the entire house. His wife Meg did her best, warm milk, soothing tea, back massage, passionate lovemaking. Everything she could think of until her fatigue would close her eyes until the following morning. Kevin would lay next to her, a slow anger brewing in the middle of his soul, anger with no recipient. How do you repair a hole in your heart when only you could feel the dripping of its blood?

How can you remove the veil that clouds your existence and every moment you feel choking, tight fingers closing around your throat? How can you erase the image of a life ending at your feet? How can you wash away the smell of death that would forever coat the membrane of your nose? I killed a man, my sweet Lord; I took a life that did not belong to me. *Thou shall not kill.* Wasn't that one of your Ten Commandments that You gave for us to obey? I have disobeyed You my sweet Lord, I have failed You big time. What can I do now to get rid of all this guilt that pours all over me like stinking gutter water, black and full of sins?

The man was only twenty-one, a father of a little baby boy and the son of a woman with sad hurtful eyes that seemed to plead for mercy right through the black and white grainy pictures in the *New York Post.* His name was Jesus, how morbid, almost like a sick joke. Jesus Antonio Muñoz. It sounded like some salsa singer that makes you want to jump and dance even though you don't know the basic steps. Perhaps Mr. Caruso already knows how to sway like one of them. They called him Papo, that's what the article had said.

Papo, whatever that means. It means he was a human being, Kevin's mind announced him in the middle of the night, a human being that could've been more of a victim than the victim themselves. When did this Papo person's life turn? Where did the little boy in him graduate from water gun to the real metal missile that plays for keeps? Is our society so corrupt that it has failed to provide the basic decency in the early chapter of a child's life and makes that child grow up without any sense of dignity or pride?

Kevin slid quietly from underneath the covers and left the room for he knew that sleep would not be visiting his eyes tonight. He went down the stairs and into the living room where he plopped on the couch surrounded by the blue streaks of the moon. And there he sat contemplating about his future, a future that no longer held the fascination of the sweet exciting unknown. When the alarm clock came on screeching from upstairs, Kevin was already dressed ready to roll, his ritual routine life dictating his every move.

THIRTEEN

They had become celebrities, Kevin and his brother Ryan. The heroes of Brooklyn, Batman and Robin, the caped crusaders of Gotham City, and the two local boys who had been able to beat the bad guys. No Joker could piss on their parade. And a parade it was. Their garage became Fifth Avenue. Their own private St. Patrick's Day Parade with the proud flying colors of green, white and orange.

People came from the farthest corners of Brooklyn, from the farthest tips of Manhattan; from across the border that made Brooklyn's soil mesh into Queens. Even brave souls from the Bronx traveled to their parade as did the forgotten sons of New York City and the transplanted Staten Islanders ventured over the

Verrazano Bridge. They all wanted to see Wyatt Earp in the OK Corral.

"I know it looks like a three-ring-circus, I know...I know," Ryan said, dunking the donut in his coffee and making it disappear in his mouth. It was nice and mushy and sweet, the way he liked it. "But they all mean well, okay maybe not the lunatics that drop by just to ogle us as if we were freaks from the side-shows in Coney Island, but the good people from the neighborhood...those mean well."

"I'm just sick of it," Kevin growled, the bags under his eyes looking more like overstuffed saddlebags. "I think they're behaving like fucking vultures."

"Come on man, in a few more days everything is going to stop. Hey, the flowers and the fruit baskets stopped coming," Ryan said, trying to sound upbeat.

"Oh really...I could really see how they are stopping all right," Kevin said, pointing with his chin at a basket that had arrived that morning. He sat next to one that was opened with enough fruits and cookies to last them at least the whole week.

Ryan glimpsed at the basket as if it was the first time he had seen it. "Okay...okay, they haven't really stopped completely, but they did drop off from five baskets a day to just one. Look on the bright side, our families and friends are eating healthier now."

Kevin shook his head and swallowed his second cup of black coffee. Lately he'd been drinking more black coffee and Ryan had begun to notice, but had decided not to make a stink about it.

"Hey Kevin, I have an idea," Ryan said, dunking another piece of donut, which this time he had to use the spoon to scoop out, because it split in half and had submerged to the bottom of the cup like a diver. "Why don't we just close the shop for a few days and let's go somewhere. You know, just the two of us. If Meg and Karen want to join us that's fine, but if not we could go upstate and do some fishing or something."

"Fishing?" Kevin asked, his eyebrow going up with puzzlement. "Since when do we fish? Shit, we don't even know which end to hold the fishing rod."

"Well, we could just go to the country and do nothing but drink beer, eat and fart."

"There's too much work here," Kevin said, spreading his arms. "We can't just get up and leave, we have responsibilities to our customers."

"Hey, we could always have Jimmy and his brother-in-law keep the place running for a few days. We've done it before; shit even Mr. Caruso said that they do a better job than we do. Besides, what do we really have that's an emergency? Mr. Caruso's old gal with the bad brakes? Maybe it's about time we stop fixing that piece of junk and tell that son-of-a-bitch to finally get something that's less than forty years old."

"What is it Ryan...you think I need a vacation?" Kevin said, pouring his third cup of coffee.

"Yes, I think you do," Ryan said, never having lied to his brother. He was always honest and straight to the punch. "Meg's been telling me that you don't even sleep much and she doesn't have to tell me that. Have you taken a good look at yourself in the mirror? Man, your eyes are just two fucking water bags hanging on for dear life. Bro' you are not even eating...I'm worried about you. And what's up with this shit that lately? You've been drinking so much coffee you alone are going to balance the budget of the whole goddamn Colombian government."

Any other time a comment like that would have made Kevin roar with laughter, but he shrugged it off and gave Ryan a weak smile. Almost like a patronizing forced smile with no warmth.

"I don't know," Kevin said, rubbing his face with one hand as if trying to rearrange his features. "Let me think about it."

"What's to think about?" Ryan pressed on. "We just call Jimmy, pick the day we are going to take off, throw a few cases of beer on the back of my truck and zoom, we're out of here."

Kevin locked eyes with Ryan and they searched each other's eyes for words that their conversation didn't communicate. Kevin was the first one to break the hold as he stood up and walked towards Mr. Caruso's old gal. "Call Jimmy and see if he's available. The least I could do is fix these brakes on Caruso's jalopy. It won't be fair to let Jimmy hassle in trying to fix a car that's older than he is. Shit, sometimes I feel that Caruso's car is so old that the only way to fix that piece of shit is to get Fred Flintstone to chisel us the parts."

Ryan laughed at Kevin's joke and like a sudden burst of sun breaking through a dark, stormy afternoon, Kevin laughed as well. It was Kevin's old laugh, the one that boomed with resonance echoes and seemed to split the rafters in any place. Ryan sighed; maybe this trip was going to make everything all right. There was nothing in life that couldn't be fixed with a little rest, relaxation and a few ice cold beers under a shaded tree.

FOURTEEN

"Do you think he'll go for the idea?" Ryan asked, excited as he lifted the cover of the simmering pot, spooning a bit of sauce to taste. It needed more salt, regardless what his last check-up said about lowering his sodium. "Man I would love to have Kevin and Meg living right across the street from us. I know the girls would be jumping with joy."

"And what makes you think he'd even want to live across from us? You guys see each other every day as it is," Karen said, knowing damn well that when an idea was embedded inside Ryan's head there was not much that could be done to remove it. Ever since Ryan found out that the Lofaros were getting ready to put their house on the market, all he could think about was having Kevin and Meg move in. It bothered Ryan that his brother continued to throw his money away by renting a tiny house in Sunset Park near the Medical Center where Meg worked. Ryan wanted to approach Mr. Lofaro before he handed the house over to a greedy real estate broker. He was already calculating putting his own home equity onto the bargaining table and co-signing for Kevin.

"I'm just looking out for them, that's all honey. It would be nice to have them live on the block, close enough for barbecues. Imagine no one would need to drive home after a couple of beers and you and Meg could have all the time to do all those girly things you are always complaining you don't get do with her as often as you like."

"But have you asked Kevin?" Karen asked, chopping fresh garlic and adding it to the simmering olive oil. They enjoyed cooking together, and to think that when they got married Ryan had trouble even putting milk in his Sugar Pops cereal. "Wouldn't Kevin tell you if he had an inclination to even look to buy a house?"

"He has been complaining lately about how small his house is. And remember that Meg is secured in her nursing job, so maybe she's thinking about adding another member to the Breen family?" Ryan sprinkled more salt in the sauce and tasted it, thought for a second and dropped half a teaspoon of pepper. "Besides, now might be the best time. I think after what happened we need to be as close to Meg and Kevin, especially Kevin. He's still not himself yet."

"Poor thing," Karen said, adding chopped onions to the garlic and oil and sautéing the ingredients. "God, I can't imagine what something like that could do to someone. It must have been very traumatic."

Karen let the wooden spoon slip from her hands to the floor as she turned to Ryan with tears in her eyes and crumbled into his arms. She sobbed uncontrollably. Finally when she was able to compose herself she spoke again. "My God, to think that you guys were in such danger. You both could have been killed. Thank God, Kevin was able to take that gun away."

Karen lost it and her tears mixed with a tremor that shook her. It was still Ryan's and Kevin's secret about the real story of the gun. Nobody knew that it was Kevin's gun and that was a story that both brothers would take to their graves.

Ryan rocked Karen in his arms, kissing the soft spot behind her ears, the area where fine little hairs curled like ribbons. "Nothing happened to us," he whispered, kneading her trembling shoulders. "God was looking out for us that day. Hush, sweetheart, hush—everything is okay."

They stood pressed against each other, heartbeat to heartbeat, soul to soul, as the aroma of spices and oil swayed above their heads.

FIFTEEN

The bartender leaped over the counter when he saw Kevin walk in. He bear-hugged him and lifted him off the floor and turned him around in a complete circle. He put him down and squeezed the back of Kevin's neck with a grip that could have crunched steel.

"How the hell are you doing you son-of-a-great-mother?" Mickey the bartender hollered, as he pushed Kevin into a stool and ran back behind the bar. Without waiting for Kevin to order, he dropped a napkin in front of him and set down a cold frosty bottle of Killian's Red beer. It was Kevin's favorite, aside from the occasional pint of well-poured Guinness Stout.

"Where's your no-good troublemaker brother?" Mickey asked, wiping his hands with a white hand

216

towel, swinging it onto his shoulder where it sat like a wrinkled scarf.

"He should be here any second, he's looking to park his truck. I stole the only spot open on the block," Kevin said, tilting his head back and letting the cold beer go down. It felt smooth, rich, and freezing cold, the way the first swallow of beer is supposed to taste after the end of a hard day's work.

"I'll be back, lad. Got to keep the brew flowing, can't pay the rent by just smacking my jaws. Just be a good man and sit there and keep the noise down," Mickey said, winking and waving his fist in Kevin's face, in good-natured fun.

"Okay, Mickey," Kevin said, lifting the bottle in a saluting gesture. "I promised to behave like the good altar boy that I was."

"Altar boy...you? Is that where you developed your taste for the pint? Sneaking and drinking the church wine for Sunday's service?"

Kevin laughed as Mickey disappeared to the other side of the bar. "Should I call you Clint Eastwood from now on?" said a wise guy voice behind Kevin,

Without turning he knew it was Frankie.

"Hey Frankie boy, how you doing?" Kevin asked, offering his hand.

Frankie took it and gave it a strong shake. He slid onto the stool next to Kevin, his ever-present bottle of Budweiser Light in hand, very seldom was it raised to his lips. It was as if Frankie only used the bottle as a prop. Perhaps it was not filled with beer, but with piss water.

"You okay?" Frankie asked in his familiar fast pattern speech. "You look like the boys from Bensonhurst took you for a little dance behind the alley."

"Just tired," Kevin said, pouring the last drops of beer down his throat. "I just need a few days off. I'll be fine."

"So what are you waiting for? Close the damn shop and go somewhere and get laid," Frankie said. It was his typical advice. He thought that all the problems of the world and the little ones in between could be resolved by a good trashing between the covers. "I have a place by Sullivan County upstate

New York. You could go there and do whatever you want, but bury fucking bodies in the backyard."

"Thanks, Frankie," Kevin said, glancing at the front door, wondering what was taking Ryan so long. "As a matter of fact, me and Ryan were talking about taking a few days off and heading somewhere to just chill out."

"Great, so it's settled. I'll drop off the keys tomorrow by the shop with the instructions on how to get there," Frankie said, surveying the area, an old habit. "You bozos fish? There's a stream behind my property packed with huge bass. They practically jump out of the water into your lap and give you a blowjob. You don't even need a license to fish there."

Kevin chuckled; Frankie had a way with words. "Good. When Ryan comes in I'll tell him, maybe we could head out there this weekend."

"Yeah, leave Friday afternoon. There's nothing better to wake up to on a Saturday morning than to the sound of nature, rather than some asshole's boom box rattling your ears with that fucking rap music. You guys will love it there, stay the whole week, the shelves are always packed with canned stuff. Just bring your own brew. I'm not that generous."

Kevin waved the empty bottle at Mickey, who was still on the other side doing exactly what he told Kevin he couldn't afford to be doing—flapping his jaws. There was nobody in the world that could flap his jaws better than he could. He made his way toward Kevin, but not before stopping here and there to chat with patrons. The regulars always felt special if Mickey addressed them by their first names, it gave them a sense of camaraderie.

"I guess you already made the rent money," Kevin said, as he took the fresh bottle from the heavyset bartender. "Cause the brew stopped flowing and the bullshit started rising."

"Do you hear that, Frankie?" Mickey asked, putting his right hand over his heart as if getting ready to pledge his allegiance to the flag. "A snot-nose like him insulting the likes of me...me a respected man...a working man. What is this world coming to? I should pick him up by his skinny pimply ass and throw him out like the common freeloader that he is. Here I am almost bottle-feeding him for free and he goes out of his way to bad mouth me. I'll tell you, Frankie...what's a man like me supposed to do?"

Frankie winked at Kevin and then leaned forward and grinned at Mickey. "I suppose you should stop the bullshit and keep the brew flowing like a good man behind the bar should."

Kevin laughed and stuck his tongue out at Mickey like a spoiled kid that just got his way. Mickey whipped the towel from his shoulder and slapped Frankie on top of his head. "You two good-for-nothing juvenile delinquents are lucky I'm a religious man. Otherwise I'd take the two of you clowns outside and give you what your daddies never gave you when you were bratty lads."

"And what did our daddies never give us...a pony?" Frankie burst out laughing as he turned and slapped Kevin's arm. "Ain't life grand? We're both getting ponies."

Mickey rolled his eyes upward and started walking to the other side where a group of friends needed a refill on their empty pitcher before continuing a competitive dart game. "Unbelievable, I have Dean Martin and Jerry Lewis here performing for free."

Kevin gulped half the bottle in one single tilt back as he fidgeted with the napkin that served as a coaster and looked nervously around. "Frankie," he said, turning sideways, as if trying to build a wall of flesh for complete privacy in the bar that was beginning to get packed with the regulars after a long day's work from their hard labor jobs. "I need a favor."

Frankie leaned forward adding another wall of flesh for more privacy. It was a damn good skill he had, able to box out anyone in the crowded area. "Shoot."

Kevin took a quick swill from the beer. "I need another gun."

Frankie's face remained rigid, no emotions were shown. He was the type of person you wouldn't want to play poker with. "I don't know if I should do that."

"Why not? You got me the first one and thanks to you me and Ryan are still alive."

Frankie sighed. "Yes Kevin, but you have to understand an illegal gun that's responsible for a killing tends to raise a lot of eyebrows. I'm feeling a bit of heat as it is from my people. You know what I mean?"

Kevin scratched his cheek and exhaled a breath that seemed he had kept in his lungs since he had walked into the bar. "I understand, Frankie...but I'm scared. I feel now more than ever that I need another piece...for protection. God knows what kind of people that punk knew that are planning some kind of revenge."

"And if something happens again, Kevin?" Frankie lifted the bottle of beer to his mouth and took a sip; enough to just moisten his lips. "Then what? The first time the cops didn't turn up too many stones. They figure you did them a whole lot of service and legwork, forget about the paperwork you saved them from doing. Even the media jumped on the good story of two innocent hardworking Irish boys going against two punks. But if the same shit happens again...the cops are going to drill you until you sing to them and Kevin. I don't need no one to sing a song with my name as part of its catchy chorus."

"Don't worry about it." Kevin finished the beer but kept it in his hand. It was a neat trick he developed to fool the bartenders. When they see a patron holding on to the beer bottle they assume that there's still beer left in the bottle, so they leave you alone. That way it made him stay away from drinking those two or three extra beers that always get you into trouble. "You should know me better than that, I'm not a squealer."

Frankie took another sip of his beer and that worried Kevin. He had never seen Frankie take two sips of beer in less than ten minutes. "I'll tell you what...when I stop by the shop tomorrow to drop off the keys for my place upstate you'll know my answer. Deal?"

Frankie stuck his hand out to establish that the conversation was finished. Kevin took the offered hand and shook it, and just like a movie script Ryan entered the bar.

SIXTEEN

Kevin pulled into the narrow driveway and killed the engine. From his angle he could see the lights in the house were off and he tried to remember if Meg had mentioned any plans she had after work. Then again he realized today was her day off from the hospital. He sat in his truck and looked at the dark interior of the small house and knew that sooner or later he had to make a decision about moving to a bigger place. Instead of rent money that was making someone else rich, he could get his own home and build a nest for the future. He knew that now with Meg's full term at the hospital, the extra money would definitely help with the mortgage payments and they could proudly claim they owned a home, with the bank of course.

He moved his neck from side to side feeling the tight knots attempting to loosen up. He slid out of the truck and climbed the four steps that led to the front door. Rolled into the handle of the screen door were a few circulars from local stores boasting some end-of-the-year sales, he quickly grabbed them and threw them inside a small garbage can next to the entrance.

Meg had put that garbage can there specifically for those uninvited circulars that many times ended up in gutters or all over the neighborhood, unread. Kevin unlocked the door and walked in. He was right about the lights. They were off and from the dining room entrance he could see the flickering of candles. They cast elongated shadows along the opaque walls.

He could smell the aroma of something delicious coming from the kitchen and knew exactly what it was, his favorite dish. Beef stew in thick gravy loaded with carrots and large chunks of red potatoes. He couldn't smell what other dishes were going to accompany the meat, but he could bet his life that it was going to be wild rice and tons of asparagus drenched in butter. A sultry instrumental sound floated from the speakers that he had hooked up all over the house.

Meg must have been hiding and waiting because the second he stepped into the candlelit room she threw herself into his unexpected arms. Her kiss was wet and full of passion, a kiss that left nothing to be desired, but had the promise of things to come. She pushed him against the wall, her fingers running through his hair and pulled his head forward in order to push his lips tighter against hers. She was in control, her body releasing a heat that was hard to resist and Kevin was trapped in her web.

She was the black widow and he the more-than-willing mate happy to die for her lust. She dug her nails into his skin and scratched his back from the top of his neck all the way down to his buttocks, up and down as if she wanted to explore every muscle along his back.

Meg was wild, a tigress searching for the magic of the moon in the deep primitive wilderness of unknown jungles. "I want to give you a son," she murmured in his ear, while licking and biting and sucking the edge of it. "Oh...oh...oh, baby, I love you. Help me give you a son."

Kevin held Meg tight, his arms around her waist and his lips smeared with her lipstick. It tasted like a cherry ice in the middle of summer. Their tongues met, again and again, twisting and welding together like alien life forms in search of a way to become one. He tasted her breath, the moistness that was around her tongue and he moaned loud and uninhibited. My God, he wanted to shout, he never wanted anything more in his life than having her now.

Now, right here and now. He lifted her in his arms, against her protest that she was too heavy. He wanted to carry her up to the bedroom, carry her up the steps like some rejuvenated Rhett Butler carrying Scarlett O'Hara from a scene straight out of *Gone with the Wind*. He felt his back tighten and wanted to laugh and yell at his aching back, *"Frankly dear, I don't give a damn,"* but he wanted her now and the room was too far, too distant. Not practical for the passionate moment, so he placed her gently on the couch and kissed her again. He was hungry, hungry for her, hungry for the normal life he had somehow lost. But now it was coming back. He wanted that life back so bad, as bad as he wanted Meg.

Kevin ripped off his clothes in a mad delirious rush and turned and helped Meg remove hers. But there was not that much to take off. Meg only wore a cute little cotton dress with nothing underneath. As the stew simmered and the carrots softened along with the red potatoes and the candles flickered in their own non-musical dance, Kevin made love to Meg like he had never had made love to her.

When they finished, bathed in their sweat and passion juices, Meg touched her stomach and prayed. "Please Lord, make him be a boy. Make him to be just like his wonderful father, make him to be the next Kevin Breen."

SEVENTEEN

The first thing that Ryan noticed was the music. It was loud and alive. He recognized Bono's powerful voice leading U2 into a monster beat. He found Kevin trying to keep up with the lyrics of the song in his God-awful Bono interpretation. If Bono were there he would have sued Kevin for deprecatory misrepresentation and would have thrown the radio out the window.

The second thing that Ryan noticed was that Kevin was in the office, and that revelation was a great sign. Ever since the disaster with the robbers, Kevin had kept away from the second floor landing. Finding Kevin here singing badly like the old days was the best thing to greet Ryan so early in the day.

"Yo' Kevin," Ryan shouted, waving the bag from Dunkin' Donuts. Today he had bought four delicious huge bowties, two for each. They were the best things to dunk in the coffee as the bowties held together much longer than a regular donut. "Jesus Christ...you sound like a dog that got his dick caught in a meat grinder."

Kevin gave him the finger and took a charger from a power drill and began using it as a microphone. He started bellowing even louder, drowning U2 and then he attempted to dance, ignoring the fact that he couldn't. If a bad dancer had two left feet, then Kevin had two left feet and two left legs as well. Ryan didn't know which was worse, his brother's singing or his brother's dancing.

Ryan put the bag of donuts on the table next to the computer and grabbed a broom that was leaning behind the door of the office. He began to play phantom guitar. He joined in singing the chorus with Kevin, with the few words that were able to pop into his memory. Neither brother had a clue as to when the song finished, for when they stopped howling there was a commercial about aspirins on the radio. How appropriate, Ryan pointed out as Kevin grabbed the coffeepot and took it downstairs. Yes, Ryan thought, just like the old days when the Breen brothers were ready to kick some ass.

"Did Jimmy call?" Kevin poured the first cup of coffee and took a bite of one of the sugarcoated bowties as they sat around the table overlooking the garage entrance. A cool breeze was coming in; there was a forecast of rain. Kevin sank his teeth again tasting the freshness of the sweetness and took a gulp of black coffee to wash it down. "We need to know if he's available to start tomorrow morning or later on the afternoon."

"Everything is set, man," Ryan said, dunking the bowtie in the coffee and then swallowing almost half of the doughy pastry. "He'll be here tomorrow early in the morning. When do you want to leave, this evening or early tomorrow?"

"What's today? Thursday? I figure we could head out tomorrow during the day. That way we make sure that Jimmy is all set and we won't hit any traffic going upstate," Kevin said, his first bowtie already gone and already on his second cup of black coffee. "Frankie should be coming by with the directions on how to get there and according to him it should be no more than an hour-and-half."

"Good," Ryan said, taking his time dunking the bowtie. Ever since he was a child he had favored dunking anything that he ate with something to drink. From those beloved Oreos cookies and milk to the most bizarre things like Barbecue potato chips dunked in orange soda. "That was cool of Frankie to offer us his place. I didn't even know he had a place. That man is a bag full of surprises."

"That's his hunting hideaway," Kevin said, licking his fingers. The best part about finishing two bowties was licking the sweet sticky sugar from your fingers. "All his buddies head out there during hunting season."

"He hunts?" Ryan asked, starting on his second bowtie. He offered half to Kevin and when Kevin declined he smirked like a little kid finding a dollar on his way to school. "I always thought that all he did was stay in the shadows of the bar trying to be the best gangster wannabe."

Kevin chuckled, pouring another cup of coffee. "Hey, he might be small potatoes compared to the big boys in the fancy expensive suits, but he still has a little push. Do not underestimate a man like that. He's more dangerous than the ones on top. He still has to prove himself that he is ready to be fitted for a silky goomba suit."

"I talked to Karen about our little trip. She thinks it's great...you think we should bring them?"

"I know Meg can't make it. She has the whole weekend shift in the hospital...besides when was the last time we went somewhere together?" Kevin pushed the empty cup aside and leaned back on the chair like a satisfied customer after breakfast at Denny's.

Ryan stopped his dunking and looked at Kevin, concentrating on the question. "Bro', the last time we ever went somewhere together, just the two of us was...shit man, I don't remember."

"Damn for someone younger than me you are definitely going senile," Kevin said, shaking his head. "Don't you remember...that summer mom thought it would be nice for us to go to camp?"

"Oh shit...you're fucking right," Ryan said, exploded with laughter. "That shit was so awful I think my mind pushed that memory out. Oh God...that was the lousiest time I ever had in my life."

"I know...remember I slept on the cot next to you. I had to listen to your annoying crying every fucking night. 'Mommy, mommy, mommy'," Kevin said, mimicking the voice of a scared little kid crying.

"Get the fuck outta here...I never cried in that place. Boy how easy people forget. Who the hell came to your rescue when that fat boy from Arkansas or whatever hick state he came from was on your ass? Man the fat boy was whipping your butt until I jumped on his back."

Kevin was laughing now, shaking his head in denial. "Shit man...you are going senile. I was the one that took the fat boy off your ass. I thought he was going to fuck you like one of his sheep back in his farm."

Ryan was roaring now, his half-eaten bowtie lying on the cellophane paper next to the cup of coffee. "Jesus, that place was awful. Mom thought she was doing us a favor but she nearly traumatized us for good. That experience almost left us brain-damaged. Man...remember when we came back home, the first thing we did was run to the playground to feel concrete and broken glass under our Converse sneakers. Fuck that grass and faggot-ass lake. We're from fucking Brooklyn...we don't need that bullshit of fresh air and bat-like insects biting us on our pale skinny legs."

"Poor mom," Kevin said. "When she saw our bodies with all those swellings from insect bites and the dried scabs on our legs she thought they switched her little boys with lepers. I'm surprised she didn't drag us to St. Mary's to have the priest bathe us with Holy water. Boy she crossed herself more than the Pope would ever cross himself in a lifetime."

"And poor dad," Ryan said, holding his stomach from the pain of laughing. "He felt so bad that every time he saw us he gave us a buck to get candy. Even his money for his weekly pints he was wasting on us. I did my best to pass by him every second possible. It was a sure buck every time. You did the same right?"

"Did the same?" Kevin asked, roaring now. "Man, that summer I think my mouth was one giant cavity. I'm surprised I didn't develop diabetes with all the candy I ate. Mr. Leo from the candy store became our best friend that summer, that's for sure."

It felt good to laugh. Didn't someone claim that laughter was the best medicine? Or didn't a school song make you believe that when you are laughing the whole world laughs with you? To Kevin both claims were true. There had been a cloud, a dark brooding cloud, which had settled on top of him since the day he pulled that trigger. But now slowly that ugly hideous cloud was turning into nice fluffy whiteness, a pillow that invited him to lie down and dream sweet loving dreams.

His brother Ryan was his life, his guiding light all along that kept him floating away from the nasty currents that tried to pull him into troubled waters. Ryan was the halcyon sea with cool lapping blue waters. His brother was his best friend, and for that Kevin thanked God a million times. It was great laughing together and now they were looking at a few days out there in the boondocks of upstate New York, which he knew would guarantee more laughter.

Slowly, but damn surely, Kevin knew he was coming out of his self-imposed funk and very soon life would be normal again. He thought about Meg and the fabulous, no it was not fabulous, but more like mind-boggling, passionate night that they'd had. My God, Kevin thought, how much he loved that woman. After they made love, they rolled on the floor and did it again.

When they finally ate dinner, their faces were still moist with perspiration. The dinner was too good for any king in any empire. She even made dessert, little cupcakes filled with cherries and strong Irish coffee that made all his hairs stand up. Then they showered, each one taking turns lathering the other's body. Then they threw themselves on the bed and dried each other, not with towels, but with their tongues and caressing hands. They made love again and again, until exhaustion set in and took them to the land of dreams.

A horn broke Kevin's thoughts as a car rolled in with its shiny chrome blinding them for a second; it was Jimmy. He jumped out before the car had settled next to Mr. Caruso's old Plymouth. "What the hell are you guys doing?" Jimmy asked, yelling as he made his way to them. "Lacking off so I get stuck with all the work?"

"How the hell are you, Jimbo?" Kevin said, meeting him halfway and embracing him. "It's been a long time I haven't seen your ugly mug."

"You know me, running all over the place wheeling and dealing," Jimmy said, accepting Ryan's embrace. Jimmy spent most of his time traveling from auction to auction purchasing cars that had been involved in minor accidents. He would fix them as good as new and sell them for a nice profit. He was such a perfectionist mechanic that he was not afraid to give his customers warranties that beat those of the original dealers. "Hey fellows, I didn't know you guys were also in the junkyard business," Jimmy said, pointing at Mr. Caruso's old gal.

Both Ryan and Kevin burst out laughing, leaving Jimmy standing there staring at them as if he was a latecomer that missed the joke and caught the tail end of the punch line.

"Well, we thought we'd give you a test before we hand you the keys to this prestigious repair shop," Ryan joked. "If you could make this car run like new the keys are yours."

Jimmy paced around the old car, hitting the tires and lowering himself to take a peek under the carriage. He stood up again and began walking to his car as he called out: "I'll be seeing you guys. If I see Jesus Christ on my way out I'll tell him that there's another Lazarus waiting to be raised from the dead."

All three broke down into hearty laughter; each patting the top of Mr. Caruso's car as if it was the geek of the class that had no idea the joke was on him.

"Seriously guys, what the hell is this?" Jimmy asked, wiping his hands on the leg of his pants, an old mechanic's habit of always thinking that his hands needed to be wiped off.

"This my friend if you really want to know," Kevin said, lifting his hand over the car as a game show host showing off the grand prize if you guessed the three right prices of a set of luggage and two cans of beans. "It's Mr. Caruso's old gal."

"Who the fuck is Mr. Caruso? The fucking opera singer from Italy that dressed liked a clown? I thought he died!" Jimmy snickered.

"No man, not the opera singer. Mr. Caruso is this old guy from the neighborhood that I think wants to be buried in this piece of junk when he dies. Almost every week he brings the car for something or other. I don't know...maybe he likes us," Ryan said.

"Or maybe he figures this is the best way to avoid moving the car from side-to-side on alternate days. Leave the piece of junk here and just pick it up only when he wants to use it. And by the looks of it I don't think it's too often," Jimmy said, shaking his head at the brothers and adding: "You guys been had. The old man has his own garage for gratis."

Ryan and Kevin looked at each other in disbelief. "Motherfucker," Kevin said, exhaling. "You might be fucking right. What a sneaky little bastard...what a fucking little con."

Ryan began chuckling as he and Jimmy went upstairs, leaving Kevin standing there with his mouth open. He was still flabbergasted when Frankie strolled into the garage as quiet as his sneakers would allow him too. Frankie did not own a car since a bad accident that killed his brother five years ago when he was at the wheel, it left him car shy. From then on he was only a passenger and always in the back seat, regardless if there were one or more occupants in the car.

"Hey Kevin, close your mouth before a fly goes in there to take a shit," Frankie said, extending his hand. Only those that he considered good friends received Frankie's handshake, others only received a nod, and his enemies usually received a baseball bat on the side of their head.

"Frankie boy, you're pretty early. I wasn't expecting you until later."

"Why wait…besides I didn't know when you guys were planning to drive out there."

"We're thinking of heading out tomorrow morning. Like that we could tighten a few loose ends. Want some coffee?" Kevin asked, hoping Frankie would decline. Because if he accepted he would need to brew a fresh pot.

Frankie shook his head and looked around. "Where's Ryan?"

"Upstairs with Jimmy…you know Jimmy? The guy that helps us out every so often."

"Yes, I think I met him once or twice. I think he did some work on Mickey's car, the last time you guys took a vacation."

"He did. And ever since Mickey had been telling me how great the guy is. Enough times that I told Mickey he could deal with Jimmy in the future. You know no hard feelings, Jimmy's a good guy."

"And did Mickey call Jimmy?"

"Yes, but Jimmy very politely turned him down. He told Mickey that his friend's customers he never touched, it was a thing of principle."

"Very impressive that there's still some loyalty out on the street," Frankie said, as he pulled a brown paper bag from his waist. "Here, put this away."

Kevin took it and slipped it inside his overall leg pants pockets; the pockets were deep and roomy. It was the gun. Then changing his mind he removed it from his pocket and hid it inside a small tool chest that sat next to the stairs.

"Also here," Frankie said, giving him a key ring adorned with a pair of dice and two keys. He also handed him a piece of paper very nonchalantly, as if what he had previously given Kevin in the brown bag were some nuts and bolts from the hardware store.

Kevin read the instructions on the slip of paper, very easy route. "Just take the Major Deegan towards Albany. It should be easy to find. There are a few fishing rods as you walk in, you are more than welcome to use them. Like I said…those bass are dumb fish, they will even bite your finger if you stick your hand in deep enough. You know how to clean a fish?"

"Ryan does. He's the chef of the house. I can't even clean my own ass."

Frankie smacked his lips in amusement. "You sick bastard...anyway, let me get going. I'm a busy man...not like you ladies with so much leisure time."

"Wait till Ryan comes down. You sure you don't want any coffee?"

"I'm sure. I'm trying to cut down on that caffeine shit. The older I get the less I could fucking eat or drink."

They heard Ryan and Jimmy's footsteps as they turned towards them. "Yo' Mr. Frankieboy," Ryan said, greeting him as Frankie came closer to the stairs and extended his hand. Ryan took it and shook it. Frankie glanced at Jimmy and was about to nod when he remembered what Kevin had said about Jimmy's refusal to steal Mickey and he extended his hand as well. He admired people that knew which side to choose from, the side of loyalty or the side of greed.

"Well I'm history," Frankie said, starting to walk toward the garage door. "You guys have fun and don't trash the place. And no wild parties."

"Oh come on, man," Ryan said, putting his arm around Frankie. "And what are we supposed to tell those two buses loaded with people that are already on their way?"

"Tell them to hit the brakes and make a fucking U-turn back home."

"You're really a fucking party-pooper," Kevin added, as he walked Frankie to the door.

"Thanks a lot Frankie. I'll see you when I come back."

"Don't worry about it. Just go out there and have a good time."

"Hey Frankie," Jimmy called out. "I'm leaving too, need a ride somewhere?"

Frankie stopped and considered the offer. Then he smiled and looked at the car that was parked by the entrance. "That sounds like a good offer…this is your car?"

Jimmy nodded as he turned and gave his goodbyes to the Breen brothers, while Frankie slid in the backseat and waited. Jimmy didn't say anything as he drove away with Frankie, waving like a little kid on his way to an amusement park in the backseat of his father's car.

"Two fuckin' characters are riding in that car," Ryan said. "Well, brother should we start our vacation now? I'm so excited that I don't feel like even lifting the smallest tool in the place."

Kevin looked at Ryan, seeing the little boy he had grown up with, and wondered about the little son of the man he had killed. He smiled, trying to hide the thought, but his brother was not so easily deceived. They were that close. Because of that closeness they both had become involved with cars at an early age. They started like any normal city kids that fall in love with the smell of gas, the slippery feel of grease on their hands and the sound of a well-kept engine purring like a kitten.

With that love they enjoyed fixing any car and soon graduated to revitalizing exteriors as well. They became good, and with time they became great, and with lots of sweat and hard work they became excellent. From parking spots out on the street where they dragged their huge tool chests and set up shop. They were able to open this place, which by word of mouth had become a very profitable business. How close were they?

At family get-togethers they joked about how they even felt each other's pains and joys. Ryan would love telling people that Kevin was suffering with a major case of hemorrhoids: *cause damn Kevin, thanks to you my ass is bleeding every time I take a shit*. Or he would slide next to Meg and tell her "I enjoyed very much what you did to my brother last night."

Kevin stood in front of Ryan and feared he would see the uncomfortable dark thought that ran through his mind. The last thing he wanted was for Ryan to be upset. "Well, we should start getting ready and pack our stuff so we could hit the road early in the morning."

"You're okay?" Ryan was still a bit reluctant about the sunny disposition that Kevin tried to portray.

"Yes, I'm okay," Kevin smiled broadly, his blue eyes sparkling, trying to hide the ugly cloud that shrouded them for a second. "I'm just trying to figure out what else I can do with Caruso's piece of shit."

"Has taking it outside and burning it crossed your mind?"

"I wish I could pack the fucking trunk with a case of dynamite and watch the biggest firecracker blow it up." Kevin slapped Ryan's back and moved around his brother to stare at the car.

"Do you want me to help you?" Ryan asked, getting down on one knee and looking at where the exhausts pipe was deteriorating.

"No, I'm just going to replace the brake pads and see if the master cylinder is okay or not. But I'll tell you if it needs more than brake pads I'm taking it off the lift and pushing it to the fucking side. When he shows up I'm going to tell him this little game is over. It's time to junk this piece of useless rusted shit."

"We should have told him that a long time ago," Ryan said, getting back on his feet and brushing his hands on the side of his pants. "Why did we keep trying to keep this sorry-looking car on the road anyway?"

"I guess we are two softies that know how much this car meant to a very lonely old man," Kevin said, with a voice that almost cracked with sentiment.

"Man, this is a hazardous piece of junk," Ryan said, wanting to keep the conversation going, keep it uplifting. "You know this is an accident waiting to happen. How would we feel if this junk stalls somewhere and causes Mr. Caruso to get into a serious accident?"

"Are you kidding me?" Kevin asked, walking to the huge tool chest, the same one they had dragged all over Brooklyn in those young exciting days. "This man only drives this car from here and around the corner to the front of his house and back here. Maybe Jimmy was right. He's just trying to avoid the hassle of moving it from side-to-side on alternate days."

Ryan laughed. "Yeah, I wouldn't put it past Caruso. He must have been a hell of a character when he was in his prime. We don't even know if he has any family or not. It is funny how we take people for granted. We see the same people every day and all we see is just that person. Nothing more nothing less. We never see them as someone's son or father or brother. It's as if we see everyone like people with no lives. Pretty strange...eh?"

Kevin took a quick glimpse at his brother. "Where the hell did that philosophy shit come from? From seeing too many politically-correct television shows with the girls? Don't tell me they have you watching those corny movies with the twins from that show with the widow father and the guy that sang like Elvis Presley?"

"What show is that?" Ryan knew exactly what show it was. An awful piece of junk called "Full House" with John Stamos and the guy that hosted an amateur video show.

"You know exactly what show I mean. Remember that Allison is my buddy and she tells me everything that goes on. She missed David Cone's perfect game because the rest of the family had hogged the television to watch a rerun of "Full House."

"Aha," Ryan pointed an accusing finger at his brother. "You also watched the show too, otherwise you would have never seen the episode where John Stamos' character had a job impersonating Elvis."

They laughed, taking turns poking accusing fingers at each other's chests, as Kevin twisted his body and mistakenly landed a slap on Ryan's face. They stopped and stared at each other. Kevin's eyes were opened wide, as if in shock that his brother slapped him. "You slapped me," Kevin said, touching the side of his face trying to look upset. "Oh no way. No little brother of mine could do something like that and get away with it."

Ryan was grinning now. "I might be the little brother, but remember I was always the best fighter. Man, I was always bailing your ass out, starting with the fat boy from camp."

"Fuck outta here! You couldn't even lick a lollipop the right way," Kevin said, jumping on Ryan and grabbing him in a headlock.

Ryan struggled a bit and was able to get out and in the same swift motion lifted Kevin from the waist and pushed him into Mr. Caruso's car. "You see how easy I could manhandle you. Face it, you're a chump."

Kevin was laughing now and breathing like an asthmatic during a heat wave. "Shit man, I'm just taking it easy. I don't want to hurt you so you could run to ma crying like you always did."

Now the brothers were wrestling, each gaining and losing a hold that was more like a slippery attempt at tickling, rather than a stronghold on something. Their bodies bouncing and crashing against the old gal of Mr. Caruso. Kevin lost his footing and landed on the floor bringing Ryan on top of him. Kevin swung his legs trying to pin Ryan to the ground but Ryan was good. He had been on the wrestling team in high school.

Kevin had tried joining the team, but the second he saw the uniform they had to wear he backed away and joined the bowling team instead. One of the few things they did separately. Now Ryan was on top of Kevin, their arms looking for a place to hold and gain superiority. They were breathing hard and laughing in hysterics. Ryan had Kevin down, and before he could count to three, Kevin rolled over and took Ryan by surprise, pinning him down as he screamed the count of three with much delight. Kevin rolled off and both lay on the greased floor, laughing and coughing until their sides hurt and they could no longer move.

"There, little brother. I just whipped your butt," Kevin said, between hard breathing.

"I'm going to tell Mom," Ryan said, pretending to cry.

They began another attack of laughter and stayed on the floor for a very long time. And at that moment, Ryan did not want to go. If it was up to him he would have stayed next to Kevin all day long. Like two old men they helped each other up and walked to the table, the small eating table that Karen had once christened Breen Mountain.

They sat in silence for a long time, realizing many years had gone by since the last time they wrestled. "Jesus," Ryan said, letting out a long breath. "Man, we are too old to be doing this. Next time let's just stick to bragging about who did what when we were young."

"I agree," Kevin said. "But just remember that I kicked your ass."

Ryan put his arm around Kevin's neck with the intention of putting him in a headlock. He didn't have the strength. "I want a rematch. Not now, but one of these days."

"Anytime, little brother. Anytime you want your ass whipped let me know. I'll be more than happy to comply."

"Hey, your breath stinks. That's why you won," Ryan said, letting out a loud laugh.

"Stink my ass," Kevin said, slapping him playfully on the top of his head. "The only thing that stinks here is you. You can't fight your butt out of a wet paper bag."

Kevin put his arm around Ryan and brought him closer to him. Then he stood up and walked to Mr. Caruso's car. "Well, I have to start sometime."

"You sure you don't want me to stay and help you out?" Ryan said, offering.

"Yeah, I'm sure," Kevin said, taking a wrench from the tool case and turning to face Ryan. "We're taking your truck. If you leave now you could buy and pack the stuff we need for tomorrow."

"Okay, now what should we get?"

Kevin stopped and walked to the table. "Let's see. Get some meat. I'm not trusting whatever canned stuff Frankie has, plus there's no way in hell we are going to fish for our food. Get some steaks and a couple of burgers. A couple packs of frankfurters and some chips," he said, lifting his head as if trying to see what more they might need. "Also, don't forget the buns for the franks and burgers. Get some water and a couple of bottles of sodas and a case or two of beer. Just don't forget my Killian's. I don't want to be in the middle of some hick town having to suck on some watered-down shit."

Ryan had taken everything down on a list and reread it back to Kevin. "Is there anything more? How about some chicken cutlets?"

"If you want, you're buying it anyway," Kevin said, tapping him on the shoulder with the wrench. "That's what happens when you get your ass pinned to the ground."

Ryan grinned and shook his head as he slipped the list in his pocket. "Fair enough. Just remember you got all the tolls and one way of gas money."

"Deal, little loser of a brother," Kevin said, putting his hand out.

Ryan looked down and it was weird. He could not remember the last time they had shaken hands like two adults. They had high-fived many times while playing or watching a sports event, but never actually shook hands. Wow...never to his recollection. He took his brother's hand and never realized the calluses that coated Kevin's palms.

He looked deep into his brother's eyes, the blue eyes that drove all the girls wild when they were growing up. The blue eyes that made all the girls gravitate toward Kevin. Ryan was never jealous, he was simply in awe of his big brother. Then Kevin did something that took Ryan by surprise and would later haunt him. But he would always see it as a blessing.

Kevin put the wrench on the table, their table, the Breen Mountain that would forever go unused. He hugged him, a tight bear hug, just like Mickey's at the bar and the strength behind the embrace almost made Ryan cry. But cry for what, he had wondered, it was just a hug between two brothers. Ryan hugged him back, with more strength than he could muster. He would always remember that it was the hardest hug he would ever give to anyone in his life.

"I love you, Ryan," Kevin said. There was a shiver in his voice, like he was also about to cry. "You are my baby brother that I love very much."

"I love you too, Kevin," Ryan said, wanting to say something funny, something smart to break up the emotional charge he was feeling. But he did not. This time he had no idea why and it was not the time for a joke.

Kevin burst into one of his gigantic sunny smiles, which he had used as a weapon in his old Casanova days. When he toyed with the opposite sex. Those girls back then had no chance when Kevin Breen smiled. He embraced Ryan and planted a kiss on his cheek, told him that he loved him. It was wild, Ryan thought, even though that display of mushiness was something they never practiced when they were growing up. It seemed so perfect, so adequate at that moment. And then Kevin chased him away and shouted, as Ryan drove the truck out of the garage screaming at him that he better not forget the Killian's or he would kick his ass again.

Ryan would never see Kevin smile again.

EIGHTEEN

Kevin washed his hands in the tiny bathroom underneath the stairs. He had been on Mr. Caruso's old gal for almost four hours. It turned out to be more than just the brake pads; it was as if everything had to be rebuilt from scratch. Damn, those brakes were going to outlast the entire car. Wait until Ryan discovered what he did to repair it; he would never hear the end of it. But Kevin couldn't help it; it was one of those jobs that became personal.

He fixed one thing to find another broken, and then he fixed that too. And zap, another thing that needed replacing followed. Besides, he was having fun. Just him and loud Santana music with a bit of U2 and Mr. Caruso's old gal as a dancing partner. How the hell could he resist? With the exception of when Ryan was sick for two weeks with a bad case of pneumonia, it was one of the few times he was in the garage working alone.

Even though he and Ryan became specialists in certain aspects of car repair, which took them to work on opposite sides of the garage, just having the presence of his brother was always comforting. Now as he brushed his nails trying to remove most of the grime underneath, he thought about the emotional moment they had both shared. It was strange. They were raised in a household where emotions were not readily displayed.

Their father a proud hardworking construction man was shaped by the old ways of Ireland. Hard worker, hard drinker, good provider. Tender moments were few and far between. Their mother was a saint, but raising a family and holding a few odd jobs cleaning offices at night made her tough as nails. But a softy inside, which she only showed in private moments. Well, he thought, just like the brothers that was a private moment. It's not like they were hugging and throwing kisses at each other in the middle of fucking Grand Central Station during rush hour.

He inspected his hands and they were pinkish and swollen, but clean enough to share a bowl of chips with a stranger at a bar. He dried them and turned off the light fixture that swung along the side of the wall. He stepped out. It was already a quarter to five and the best thing to do was to get his stuff ready, close the place down and head back home. He was looking forward to a restful nice sleep and the scenic drive tomorrow to the cabin or whatever type of place Frankie had upstate.

He had no clue of what to expect, but he was sure he was going to be surprised. With Frankie what you saw was most certainly not what you were going to get. Shit, Kevin chuckled under his breath. We might find ruffled curtains on the windows and handmade dollies all over the tables with fresh-cut flowers in a vase positioned where the sun would hit it just right. A lovely faggot picture according to his book.

He climbed the stairs and halfway up he climbed back down. Knelt on one knee by the small tool case that was kept there. Opened the lid and took the gun out; it was best to keep it inside the safe like the last one. The last thing he wanted was for Jimmy to find it. He went back upstairs and hesitated for a second before entering. He knew that it was going to take him awhile to get used to what occurred inside the oversized closet they called office. Took a deep breath and went in, trying to avoid the spot where the dead man had fallen like a rotten tree.

He walked slowly to the safe, yet somehow he couldn't do it. It was as if his legs decided that it was best to stay away from that spot if possible. Damn, he shouted in a soft yell, what the hell is wrong with me? Why should I feel like this when all I did was protect what was mine and saved the life of my brother and perhaps my own. He sat down on the chair that was always pushed underneath the table with the old computer and lowered his head to his hands and stared at the place where one lousy second changed an entire lifetime.

He felt his breath coming out choppy, as if air decided not to enter and all he had for survival was the bit of oxygen still inside his lungs. Felt a nervousness creeping upward into his heart and it felt as if something was holding it, squeezing it. Was this how anxiety attacks started? Or could it be how those so called unexpected heart attacks jump on your ass and slam you hard against the ground, leaving you to die foaming at the mouth like some mad dog.

Kevin wanted to get away, even better, he wanted to run. Dash out of that evil place and not come back. But something pulled him to stay still, something keeping his ass…or as Uncle Billy said…his arse, glued to the damn chair. He felt sweat, cold sweat, wetting his face. But when he reached and touched his forehead there was no moisture, just a cold clammy feeling. Like touching a fish that's been dead for a few hours.

"Jesus," he mumbled. And Uncle Billy's voice was what he heard instead. Jaysis. He turned and felt like the point of a compass seeking its way back home. His whole body was now turned, straight like a fucking arrow, toward the safe. The safe took shape and what Kevin saw in his delirious mind was an ugly stump of a monster of rusted steel. He could have sworn he saw the safe moving inches toward him.

Thump, thump, thump. He heard the ugly hoof-like feet getting closer. *Me Jaysis, I'm a bloody fuckin' mess, I'm behavin' like an arse.* That was Uncle Billy's voice, which Kevin heard again in his mind instead of in his own heavy Brooklyn-accented voice. He closed his eyes tight and felt his body tremble, the way it used to shake when he knew his father was coming home and he had done something wrong. But why was he trembling?

He had not done anything wrong. On the contrary, what he had done was right. All he did was send some evil crippled soul to hell. The damn punk deserved everything he got, especially that close range bullet between his eyes that exploded and sent half his teeth and part of his brain right into Kevin's mouth. We became one, you motherfucker, Kevin screamed at the spot where Papo had died.

"I got to get the hell out of here," Kevin yelled at himself. "Come on. What's so hard about pushing your lazy good-for-nothing arse away from the table and onto your feet? Come on, lousy trainee. On your feet and up. One-two-three-march…march out of here and to your fucking house where Meg was waiting for another sex marathon billed the Second Coming of Kevin Breen."

He was getting spooked out of his mind and that wasn't sitting right with him. He opened his eyes and bit down on his lower lip, hard enough to bring out the taste of blood. That seemed to wake him up. The equivalent of a good roundhouse slap to bring his ass — or wasn't it arse? — back to his senses. He laughed a weak laugh and he needed a drink. He did not need a cold refreshing beer, nor a dark foamy pint, but a real drink.

A hard fucking nasty-ass-burning drink. The type of drink that makes you shit-faced with three strong ones. On an empty stomach, two would knock your brain off your skull. There was a bottle in the small table where he brewed the coffee in the morning. Thank you, Meg, for that lovely garage-warming gift. The pot once shiny and white was now dull and splattered with old grease stains that defeated the efforts of any soap or cleanser.

Kevin opened the drawer and a bottle rolled to the front. It was a bottle of Bacardí, Puerto Rican rum. It was a leftover from a time when his old buddy brought him those delicious meat pies during Christmas. His friend Peter had brought the bottle as he had said, "To teach you Irish cats that there's more than black beer and scotch". The bottle was almost full, after two shots each, both had realized they were not drinking men, so they settled on a six pack of Heineken.

Kevin took the bottle and unscrewed the top. Before he took a sip he laughed. Puerto Rican rum, how goddamn appropriate. The best weapon to fucking exorcise a Puerto Rican ghost. He took a swill and the warm liquor scraped his throat. It was like sending millions of sharp shaving blades down his esophagus. It made his entire body shake with tiny convulsions.

He was about to take another shot and put the bottle away to run back to Meg's soft freckled arms, but something caught his eyes. Underneath the safe something red peeked at him. He went closer and focused on it. The corner of a Polaroid. He bent down and grabbed the photograph and pulled it out. It was the picture of a baby, and Kevin knew, just who the baby was. He took the picture to the table along with the rum.

He sat, his eyes never leaving the big-eyed baby that stared soulfully at him. Kevin threw his head back and swallowed a mouthful of liquor. He grimaced at the bitter taste, but swallowed some more. The bitterness began to taste better and soon it would taste like strong Chinese tea. He traced his index finger through the captured image of the lovely child dressed in light blue—or was it powder blue?—like the cans of Sea Breeze air-freshener Meg was fond of.

"Who are you little boy?" Kevin asked the picture. "Who will you become? Do you miss your Daddy tickling you in the morning? Or kissing you at night? Do you miss him at all? I killed your Daddy, little boy."

Little boy blue like the famous painting he once saw at the Metropolitan Museum of Art during a school trip with Ms. Abel's class. Who will teach you how to play catch in those early cold mornings of April before the baseball season starts? Was he a good Daddy, little boy? Little boy blue. Could you forgive me, little boy? Could you ever forgive me for taking your Daddy away from you, my sweet little blue boy?

Kevin took another shot of rum, some trickling down his chin and into the open collar of his overalls. He placed the picture down in front of him where he could see it, as if it was the real baby lying in his crib. Why God? Why, did You do this to me? How can I live the rest of my life having to carry not just the burden of a dead man's weight, but the weight of a future that I killed as well?

He closed his eyes and felt tears welling up and when he opened his eyes again they cascaded down, washing away the taste of rum from his face. He began to sob, his shoulders shaking up and down as his lips quivered and made his teeth chatter in a lonesome song. Kevin dropped his face into his hands and wailed like a lost child, perhaps like the lost child that the little blue boy has become.

"Motherfucker!" he shouted, making him hoarse. "You stupid motherfucker! Why did you leave this baby boy alone and come into my life to be killed?"

Kevin stood up and walked around, his shuffled steps scraping the floor as if he had become the black-and-white Frankenstein from the late, late show. He came to a sudden halt, right on the same exact spot where he had stood that day and made his brave stand. Had it been brave or dumb? BOOM! He could still hear the shot and could feel the powerful vibration that climbed through his forearm and into his shoulder when the gun went off.

No, the gun didn't go off, he'd pulled the trigger. He had squeezed with all his might and then he smiled. A smile or a grin? Did it really fucking matter what he did? He remembered the face, the angry face that was yelling at him and caved in like a basketball that had developed a leak. And then it exploded, BOOM!

Like a giant cyst, which someone squeezed and everything came out flying with force, puss and all. Kevin had tasted the taste of a dead man's soul and had tried to not swallow, but it happened so fast that something went down. Perhaps it was the spirit of a desperate man that came to rob him, but Kevin robbed him instead. Robbed him of his fucking wasted life.

"I swallowed your ass, motherfucker. You dumb-ass spic. That'll teach you never to fuck with a fighting mic."

"Damn you!" Kevin screamed at the phantom he saw in front of him.

He dropped to his knees, his body shaking uncontrollably and felt his heart pounding, BANG, BANG, BANG, like a fist knocking on a door. He looked at the spot on the floor where Papo had died and could see blood, the pool of blood that ran like a spilled gallon of red paint. He had never realized how much blood a human head held. Or had it been every drop from head to toes?

"You son-of-a-bitch!" Kevin cried out, his tears mixing with saliva that drooled from his mouth. "Why me, motherfucker? Why fucking me?"

He pounded his fist on the floor, wishing he'd been pounding on the carcass of the stupid man. He slammed his knuckles until they bled; until every bone was shattered into an ugly grotesque mass of pain. Sprawled on the floor, his body shivering as if he was out in a cold winter night naked. Lay there until his little boy cries stopped and hiccupped sobs ripped through his throat. Lifted himself first to his knees, then to his feet, stumbling like a drunken bum back to the seat where little boy blue waited patiently for him.

Kevin took the picture in his broken bloody hands. The big eyes looked at him with what felt like passion, sadness and bewilderment. The lips were not forming a smile or a grin, but Kevin knew they were constructing words that only their hearts could hear.

"I was you once," Kevin whispered to the child. "And you will always be me, yet we are strangers. Are we? Your small hands are perfect and not scarred, unlike mine, destroyed under the hood of this goddamn lousy life. Why are you staring at me little boy? Yet I'm staring back. Are we both seeking answers to questions that do not exist? Did I just throw your future away? Or was it your father that threw it away into the gutters of his ugly vices and foolish dreams?"

A tear dropped onto the photo and he wiped it off, leaving a bloody streak.

"Why do you keep staring at me, little blue boy, without saying anything? Or did you say something and I stubbornly ignored you?"

Kevin wanted to rip his eyes away, but the big eyes kept him looking. The big eyes understood his pain. Pain that now they shared in this screwed-up world. Kevin brought those big eyes closer to his as he held the photograph in his hands.

"Your eyes are looking at me and I feel you are forgiving me for the mistake that I committed on your behalf."

Big beautiful eyes of a child that would be forever impaired by the harshness of life. Kevin let the picture drop on the table and picked up the gun. He felt the weight of it and the contrast of its form when comparing it to the picture of little blue boy.

"I cannot forgive myself, little blue boy. I took not only a life, but I took yours as well. And isn't it true what they say that everything comes in three?"

He lifted the gun and could smell oil and gunpowder. Opened his mouth and inserted it. The barrel pushing his tongue to the back of his throat. Felt his head shaking as his teeth clattered on it. The cold and oily shaft of death. He closed his eyes and opened them again. He looked at the big eyes staring at him with indifference and Kevin wondered if little blue boy was also named Jesús Antonio Muñoz. "Jesús." Kevin mumbled the name of a dead man using not the pronunciation for Jesus Christ, but the pronunciation for a Hispanic man.

"Haysus".

It sounded almost like Uncle Billy's Jaysis. Kevin closed his eyes and took a deep breath. His teeth stopped chattering on the barrel. He was calm and serene. He chanted softly, Haysus, Jaysis, and pulled the trigger with all his might.

NINETEEN

KEEEVIIIIINNN!

Ryan jumped out from a terrible dream with a shout laced with his brother's name. He shook in disoriented hesitation feeling his body drenched in sweat as he sat up and ran his fingers through his hair. He exhaled loudly and inhaled with the same force. He was gasping. Whatever dream or nightmare responsible for his trembling was a distant fog. But it was about Kevin, that he knew. He had felt it like a solid punch to the back of his throat.

He swallowed hard and could have sworn that there was a strange pain in his mouth. The same sting you feel when the dentist injects you before pulling a tooth. Ryan cleared his throat and breathed with relief thanking God that it was only a dream. Then the phone rang and he wondered if he had thanked God a bit too soon. Was he still dreaming?

The phone rang again and the ringing seemed louder than ever. It was as if the phone knew that something had to be said without much of a wait. Karen turned over, gave Ryan a sleepy disturbed glare and mumbled, "Who the hell is calling so late?"

She picked up the phone and her face lost all color, all shape. To Ryan her face became just a long twisted look of panic and horror blended into one. She dropped the phone on her lap and her lips quivered, trying to form words that refused to come out.

Ryan took the phone and brought it to his ear, still praying: *Oh Dear God, oh Dear God, let this still be part of my dream.*

The voice he heard was foreign, distant. But Ryan heard the authority it possessed. It was a voice that had many years of experience with phone calls made in the middle of the night to strangers. It said a few things, but all Ryan kept hearing over and over was something his mind refused to acknowledge. The voice paused, allowing Ryan to collect himself and Ryan wondered why and then he knew—he was sobbing, no he was yelling like a lunatic—as he kept hearing over and over. Kevin is dead.

TWENTY

It was a sea of black and white. Little kids ran around in their Sunday best oblivious to the pain of the grownups. A parade of friends and families marched solemnly past the closed casket surrounded by flowers and burning scented candles. A New York Yankees cap was hanging near the propped up Mass cards, and on a table draped in white satin was a photograph of a young good-looking man. The satin was shiny and the smile in the photograph could outshine Times Square on New Year's Eve.

It was a picture of Kevin from last Christmas when he had received Yankees season tickets from Ryan. He had nearly fainted when he opened the plain-sealed white envelope with "Merry Christmas" written in neat red letters across it.

Ryan watched the procession that passed by, acknowledging the good intentions. Yet he couldn't help but notice how surreal it all was. He saw Uncle Billy bunched together with his parents, the short stocky old man holding court and trying to keep his upper lip from quivering.

He had been Kevin's favorite uncle and now Ryan knew, Uncle Billy had Kevin's identical grin. A sly smirk that seemed to keep you guessing what it was he knew. Oh, Kevin, Ryan looked straight at the casket, the shiny, steel coffin that Meg had chosen. If it had been up to him, he would have settled for plain wood. Wood was more comforting, more real, just like Kevin—no fancy shit was Kevin's motto.

"I'll tell you what, Ryan," Kevin used to joke. "When I die and you're still around, cash the damn insurance money and skip town. Forget about a funeral and the damn vultures in their cheap black suits with their phony smiles and sissy handshakes. Leave my naked stiff butt in the fucking morgue. What the hell are they going to do? Drop me off in the gutters with the rest of the rotten garbage? I don't think so. Just leave my ass there and take the guys from the neighborhood to a Yankees game and get drunk on those overpriced beers you get at the stadium."

"What happens if you die in the winter? There will be no Yankees games," Ryan had asked.

"Well shit, I don't know. That's your fucking problem. Remember I'll be dead."

Why Kevin? How come you didn't tell me what the hell was going on? Why the fuck didn't you let me stay with you—why Kevin, why? I even bought a book that was going to teach us how to fish. I got you a case of Killian's and a pack of Guinness. Man we were supposed to go and let it all hang out. Jaysis, Kevin, you bloody eejit.

Ryan felt a soft tug on his arm. It was Mr. Caruso. The old man's eyes were red and watery. It was the first time Ryan had seen Mr. Caruso speechless. The poor man stood there, once again between the two brothers, but this time with no snappy remarks. Who could ever imagine Mr. Caruso without any dialogue?

"The last car he ever fixed was your old gal. Now you can go and learn those fancy mambo steps," Ryan said, forcing a brave smile as he felt the old man's arm wrap around his neck. He felt Mr. Caruso's suffering and loved the old man. He would always be a reminder of the good times in the garage with Kevin. But that comforting feeling of remembrance would have to wait. It was too soon to feel solace in memories.

The day went by unnoticed, as if it were mourning itself. Meg was still holding strong. Ryan hugged her once in a while. He thought he was giving her strength, but it was the other way around. She was a remarkably proud woman and Ryan wondered when she would finally crash. When would she cry? Probably in privacy, just like Kevin.

He felt for his parents who sat looking so small and old. Guests approached them and he saw the handshakes, the awkward abbreviated embraces. His father's attempt at slight mumbles, as if he did not have the energy to form a syllable.

Ryan's heart felt heavy, as if he were carrying the huge tool chest both brothers used to drag all over Brooklyn to repair cars for an honest price. It was almost time for everyone to leave and get ready for tomorrow's burial. Ryan followed Uncle Billy with his eyes, watching as he approached the heavy steel box where his favorite nephew lay.

The old man began to sing "Oh Danny Boy" in his beautiful accented Irish brogue.

When Uncle Billy finished the somber Irish song, the mourners left in tears to prepare for the following morning.

TWENTY ONE

The cars lined up as a bright blue sky fell on them like a new spring jacket bought for Easter Sunday Mass. They rode in long, black freshly waxed limousines through the streets of Brooklyn. They went through the old neighborhoods and past Mickey's bar where everyone stood outside with their heads lowered and a Guinness or Killian's raised in solemn salute. They went by the schoolyards and the sidewalks where Kevin had fallen in love with the mechanism of cars.

They drove Kevin for the last time through his beloved garage. Like an old western caravan they filed through the streets and when they turned the corner leaving the garage in their rearview mirror a last car joined in. It was Mr. Caruso's beautiful old gal and out of all the vehicles in the procession, the old gal was the one with the best brakes in town.

ABOUT THE AUTHOR

Manuel A. Meléndez is a Puerto Rican author born in Puerto Rico and raised in East Harlem, N.Y. He is the author of two mystery/supernatural novels, "When Angels Fall", and "Battle for a Soul", four poetry books, "Observations Through Poetry", "Voices From My Soul", "The Beauty After the Storm", "Meditating With Poetry", and two collection of Christmas short stories, "New York-Christmas Tales, Volume I and II". The novel "When Angels Fall", was voted by The LatinoAuthors.com as the Best Novel of 2013. While "Battle for a Soul" was awarded Honorable Mention in the 2015 International Latino Awards for mystery novels. His short story "A Killer Among Us" was published by Akashi Books in "San Juan Noir" anthology. He's working on a collection of suspense short stories, and a mystery novel. The author lives in Sunnyside, N.Y. harvesting tales from the streets of the city. For more information please visit his website.

www.manuel-melendez.com

Made in the USA
Middletown, DE
24 November 2020